LEEVA
AT
LAST

Also by
SARA PENNYPACKER

MIDDLE GRADE BOOKS

Pax, Journey Home

Here in the Real World

Pax

Summer of the Gypsy Moths

The Clementine series

PICTURE BOOKS

Meet the Dullards

Sparrow Girl

SARA PENNYPACKER

LEEVA AT LAST

Illustrations by
Matthew Cordell

BALZER + BRAY
An Imprint of HarperCollins*Publishers*

This one's for my Writer Babes, with thanks
—S.P.

To Julie, Romy, and Dean
—M.C.

CoNTE

NTs

AT FIRST

Leeva Thornblossom flew outside the instant she heard the *Nutsmore Weekly* thunk against the door. Fetching the newspaper was the only time her parents permitted her in the front yard.

Ignoring the paper, she jumped off the step and waded through the weeds to the towering hedge that surrounded her yard. There, she knelt and cautiously worked her hands into the sharp-needled branches to open a sight line. Whoever delivered the paper was long gone, as always, but her eyes swept the sidewalk and yes! She was in luck today: a woman gripping a little boy by the hand, approaching from the right.

Leeva scarcely blinked as they drew near. First, she would call out a bright *Hello!* Then, when the woman located her in the hedge, she'd add . . . well, this was the hard part. What Leeva had always ached to say to someone was, *I am here! And you are here!* But somehow those words seemed too important to call through a hedge. Besides, what would she say next?

Just as the woman reached the edge of Leeva's yard, she scooped up the toddler and crossed the street.

Again! Why did people always do this, as if avoiding an invisible barbed wire fence? Crestfallen, Leeva watched the woman hurry past on the far sidewalk, the little boy jouncing on her hip, until she was out of sight.

Better luck next week, she told herself as she plodded back to pick up the paper. There on the step, she flipped through it, looking for the "Improve Your Vocabulary" column filler—there was never any actual news in the paper, but a new word, complete with definition, every week, at least she had that. Before she found it, though, a headline caught her eye.

And Reader, for the first time ever, Leeva saw actual news: "Nutsmore Announces Opening Day of School for Children Six and Older."

Well, she practically toppled over into the doorway briars in her shock. Her town had built a school! And since she was somewhere between eight and nine—not

knowing her birthday, she had never been able to calculate her age exactly—she would be going to this school! At last, it was out into the world for her, in only—she checked the announcement—five weeks and three days.

She would tell her parents after dinner, when they were in the least rotten of the moods they simmered in all day.

"Wait, that's silly," she chided herself out loud as she ducked through the briars and went inside. Her mother was Nutsmore's mayor and her father was its treasurer. Surely they already knew about this new school.

Then why hadn't they told her?

Was it possible they were planning to surprise her? On the soap opera she watched, *The Winds of Our Tides*, the Cleverton family always made a big deal of revealing joyous news to their twin daughters: *For you, darlings! Ta-da!* Granted, this kind of parent-like behavior was wholly unlike her own mother and father, but there was a first time for everything.

It was hard to wait for them to get back from work.

Leeva solved the bookkeeping problem her father had left for her and signed it with a flourish. She sharpened the toes of her mother's shoes and rushed through the rest of her regular duties. Then she threw herself into the exercises on *Vim and Vigor at Any Age* with extra vim and vigor and turned on *The Winds of Our Tides* with a new, warm sense of connection—those twin Cleverton daughters attended school and now so would she.

Unfortunately, though, today the show opened with the scene that Leeva always dreaded. This scene was so upsetting she usually closed her eyes when it occurred. Today she kept them open.

"Bedtime!" the Cleverton parents called. When the twins scampered up obediently, the parents patted their daughters' heads and hugged those girls so tightly you'd think they were hurtling off into outer space instead of climbing into side-by-side beds, each with its own pretty quilt.

The soap opera parents squeezed those girls as if they couldn't bear to be away from them for a single night.

They squeezed them as if they were precious.

Watching it now, an odd cry accidentally escaped Leeva's throat—something between a gasp and a wail. She snapped off the television. Then she carried the

Nutsmore Weekly to her thinking spot, which was the place between two cabinets where a dishwasher used to be until her parents sold it, noticing that Leeva had grown tall enough to reach the sink.

Leeva did her best brain work in this empty spot, right from the first day it had appeared. On that day, she'd sunk to the floor in shock. If she spent, say, half an hour a day doing dishes for the next ten years, she'd be at the sink a total of—even so young, she calculated easily—109,560 minutes. Then something worse struck her: her parents had traded those 109,560 minutes of hers—minutes they might have spent enjoying her company—for only fifty dollars. *My parents don't find me very valuable*, was the depressing conclusion she'd drawn.

Today, her thoughts were more cheerful—*School! Finally out into the world!*—as she sank down cross-legged with the newspaper. Before turning to stare at the miraculous announcement again, she hunted down the "Improve Your Vocabulary" word: *Deluxe—Notably luxurious or sumptuous; of a superior kind.* The word was good enough to produce a tingle, which only happened with the best of them.

When her parents' car crunched into the driveway at 6:20, she got up. Gazing into the refrigerator, she heaved a sigh. Didn't a night like this call for a celebratory dinner, maybe even a meal for herself? But no, all she saw now was the same grim stuff she'd seen every day since her parents had decreed her big enough to prepare their food. "She hasn't made us any richer, she hasn't made us any more famous. She might as well serve us our meals!" had been their exact words.

Reader, let's pause for a moment and have a look inside this fridge to see what caused her deep sighs.

Food in the Thornblossom household fell into two categories, neither of which could be labeled *deluxe*.

Leeva's father bought only from the Cheap-O Depot Grocery Warehouse and only what was moldering on their Rock-Bottom Sale shelf. Mostly this was Cheezaroni.

Cheezaroni bore a glancing resemblance to macaroni and cheese, except that the macaroni and the cheese were indistinguishable from each other and they were both indistinguishable from the box, so even when you followed the instructions perfectly, what you ended up with was a flavorless cardboardy mash that smelled powerfully of feet. Once a month, Mr. Thornblossom had Leeva bake up dozens of these food bricks, thereby reducing the cost of turning on the oven, and stack them on his side of the fridge. He ate them night and day.

The items on her mother's side were quite different. *Celebrities This Week* magazine was filled with famous people dining on trendy dishes, and Mrs. Thornblossom purchased them all. Last week, an actor had been spotted in a restaurant smacking his lips over an eel custard with boar's knuckle jelly, and so that's what Leeva was sighing at right now.

She had managed to subsist on the leftovers from her parents' meals, but she was hungry all the time. She was hungry now, and she would be just as hungry when she fell into bed.

She prepared her parents' plates and brought them into the living room right on time, at exactly 6:40.

Two television sets blared across

the room. Leeva's father was tuned to *Money Talks!*, tapping the figures that flashed across the screen into his calculator. Her mother stared hang-jawed at *Celebrities Tonight!*

Leeva set the plates on the trays in front of them, crawling on her hands and knees so as not to disturb their viewing, and then sat on her stool in the corner to wait.

Reader, we'll take a break here, too. Regrettably, you have to meet Leeva's parents.

MONEY AND FAME

Leeva's parents cared about one thing only, and it certainly wasn't Leeva.

Well, each one cared about one thing only.

Leeva's mother cared about *FAME*. As mayor of Nutsmore, she made sure people knew who she was. "Fame is the most powerful power there is," she liked to say. When the townspeople objected to something she did, she would shoot them a glare hot enough to fry bacon. "Don't you know who I am?" she'd demand. "If you have a complaint, I will fire you. Do you have a complaint?"

No was the only acceptable answer.

Once in a while, some unlucky townsperson would make the mistake of asking, "Fire me? From what job?"

"The job of being mayored by me," was her answer. "Also, now I'm fining you a Talk-Back Tax. Stop talking and go away."

The best thing about Leeva's mother was her shoes. She had hundreds of pairs. Along with her hair, which she wore stacked in a tower, the five-inch heels gave her a powerful height advantage and a signature look. The toes, sharpened by Leeva daily, could splinter shins. The stiletto heels, specially crafted with crystal beads at the bottoms, went *clink-clink-clink* when she tottered around and *scritch-scritch-scritch* when she ground them in fury. These brittle sounds were what made the shoes the best things about her—at least people always knew when to get out of Malicia Thornblossom's way.

Leeva's father, Nutsmore's treasurer, cared only about *MONEY*. He collected gobs of it, wads of it, mountains of it from the citizens of Nutsmore. He stuffed this cash into shoeboxes (which he got for free, you can guess where) and stored it in a locked bedroom upstairs.

The best thing about Dolton Thornblossom was . . .

Actually, there was nothing good about him at all.

Reader, by now you might be wondering why these two despicably selfish human beings ever had a child.

Well, Mrs. Thornblossom, as we've seen, was

obsessed with fame. One evening, she saw a piece on *Celebrities Tonight!* about how many movie stars were having babies. *Here's Hollywood's most famous couple with their new little bundle of joy*, cooed the show's host.

"A baby is a fashion accessory that adds to one's signature look," Mrs. Thornblossom mused, checking the mirror she had hung beside her chair and patting her hair-stack. "Like a pocketbook. We'll get one."

Mr. Thornblossom's fingers hovered over his calculator. "Will it bring us more money?"

This is the crucial moment, Reader. Leeva would not exist, and therefore this book would not exist, if the answer to his question had been *No*.

But Leeva's mother, considering her husband's question, turned back to her television show for guidance. And just then, the host announced that on the very day that Hollywood's most famous couple had brought their baby home, they had signed a contract to star in a movie for more money than any actor and actress had ever been paid.

Fame *and* money, all from one little bundle of joy!

"Hunh . . . ," Mr. Thornblossom said, paying full attention now. "Okay."

And so, nine months later, Leeva was born.

Did having a child make these two any richer, any more famous? No, of course not. Only a nincompoop would have believed it would.

All right, you've heard enough. Back to the story.

LYING LIARS LIE

Once her parents had finished their dinners, Leeva positioned herself where she could address them both and cleared her throat. "Mother? Father? Do you have some news to tell me?" She stretched out her arms to welcome their surprise.

Leeva's mother, staring at her television set from her throne-like chair, commented on how notable Taffy Glamoo's new hairdo was. Leeva's father, in his recliner, jabbed his calculator keys at a determined clip.

Leeva felt her arms drop a little bit. "I'm ready for your news," she tried again.

Leeva's father hunched closer over his calculator, muttering. Her mother turned up the volume on her set.

Leeva's arms gave up. She looked down at her hands,

their nails bitten as neatly as she could manage. At the brown braids she'd carefully finger-combed falling over her faded yellow dress. After years of comparing herself to the child stars in her mother's magazines and to the twins on *The Winds of Our Tides*, she knew what a disappointment she was. Still, she did exist. How, then, could her parents act as if they didn't see her or hear her? It was a question she asked herself every time she tried to talk with them. Tonight, with the exciting news hanging in the air, it was especially vexing.

Leeva tried one more time. "Isn't Nutsmore getting something wonderful?"

Her mother finally looked up. She blew a quick kiss at her reflection in the mirror and then nodded. "Oh, yes, that. I don't know how you found out, but yes."

"Oh, thank you, thank you! I'm so excited," Leeva cried, exactly the way the twin Cleverton girls greeted all their surprises.

"You should be excited," Mayor Thornblossom agreed. "Everyone will be."

Mr. Thornblossom cast a suspicious glance over at his wife.

"I've commissioned a statue of myself," she told him. At his look of alarm, she flapped calm-down hands and added, "Paid for by the townspeople, of course."

"What?" Leeva said. "But that isn't—"

"It's a well-known fact that statues are of famous people. And famous people have statues."

"No, I was talking about—"

"Fifty feet tall. I've hired a separate sculptor for the shoes. Gold-plated, five feet high at the heels."

Leeva shuddered. Life-size, her mother's shoes were alarming enough. "But I meant *this*," she said, presenting the newspaper. "Nutsmore has a school now! And I'm going!"

"You're not going," Mayor Thornblossom said with breathtaking finality. She had a lot of practice decreeing that people couldn't do things, and it showed.

"But it says here, all children six and older are expected to attend grades one through twelve, in five weeks and three days."

Mr. Thornblossom dropped his calculator. He stroked his mustache. "Six. One. Twelve. Five. Three. Those are numbers! Numbers are essential for counting money."

"That's true, Dolt," Leeva's mother agreed. She began to tap a stilettoed heel. *Clink-clink-clink.* "But Leeva's not going," she repeated even more firmly. "She already knows numbers. You remember—she works them for you."

This was true. One evening, three years before, her father had been stewing away, trying to solve a simple 3 percent dividend yield out loud, when Leeva had grown impatient and supplied the answer. Since then, Mr. Thornblossom did his own adding and subtracting—he could handle those with his calculator—but anything more difficult he turned over to Leeva, and each morning, he left her a bookkeeping problem to solve.

"But I *want* to go," Leeva tried.

Her father picked up his calculator. Her mother zeroed in on "Famous in a Flash," the final segment of *Celebrities Tonight!*, during which an ordinary person was plucked from obscurity and given a ten-year contract to live in Hollywood as a reality star. Mayor Thornblossom both loved and despised this segment. "It should be *me*," she muttered, as she always did. "*I* should be made famous in a flash."

"Wait." Leeva looked from one parent to the other. "You weren't surprised there's a school. You already knew. Why didn't you tell me?"

Her parents shrugged at each other. *Why should we?* the shrugs seemed to say.

"How long?" Leeva's voice quavered. "For how long has there been a school in Nutsmore?"

More shrugging. *Since always, big deal, who cares?*

"But you always said schools were only in soap operas. That real towns didn't have them." Leeva staggered backward as the truth struck her like a bowling ball to the chest: Her parents had *lied* to her.

Now, Reader, Leeva had known her mother and father were liars, of course. According to the stories they told each other at night, lying was pretty much all they did in their jobs. It was how they'd gotten their jobs, in fact: *Vote for us! We promise this, we promise that!* But it had never occurred to her that they would lie to *her*, their own daughter.

Learning that you cannot trust the people you've relied on is devastating—like discovering that what you thought was solid earth below your feet was actually a nest of spider bones. Leeva was shaken to her core.

But at the same time, like a rabbit sensing a wolf, she felt all of her senses quicken. Her eyes and ears crackled with new acuity. Her skin began to zizzle as if electrified.

From this moment on, she realized, she must be extremely cautious around these two liars. She must sharpen her wits and be prepared to act with boldness and laser-like speed.

THE QUESTION

Leeva took a step away from her parents. "Why?" she asked coolly. "If you knew there was a school, why haven't you ever sent me?"

Her mother scowled. "School teaches those subjects . . . Human, human . . . Human Inanities. Music, la-di-la, literature-shmiterature, poetry-shmoetry, art. All that nonsense."

"Nonsense," her father parroted. "You only need to learn numbers. So you can make us money."

"She knows her numbers, Dolt," her mother reminded him again. "But yes, money is important. Money can get you fame." She gave her husband a sly wink. "And fame can get you money."

Leeva thought of the locked bedroom directly above

them. The shoeboxes came in, but they never went out. "But what is the money *for*? What are you going to *do* with it?"

"*Do* with it?" Mr. Thornblossom's brow furrowed. "If I *do* something with it, I won't *have* it."

"But if you don't do anything with it, it's only greenish paper in a box. I don't understand why you want it."

"That's because you're not a genius like me," he said, tapping his forehead.

Just then, both television programs ended. Leeva had only a few moments of her parents' attention before the next ones began. She drew herself up to her full height. "I don't care if they only teach those Human Inanities. I want to go to school and be with other people."

"*People?*" her parents shrieked at once.

"You think *people* are more important than money and fame?!?" her mother demanded.

"You asked what *money* is for!" her father cried. "Well, then what are *people* for?!? Ha! Answer that!" His eyes gleamed in triumph, as if it had been quite an accomplishment, turning her own question around on Leeva.

"People are for being famous to," Mrs. Thornblossom declared. "Obviously. You can't be famous without people."

Mr. Thornblossom added one of his rare thoughts. "And to get money from. That's all they're for."

Leeva felt certain that people were for more important things than getting money from and being famous to. Why else would the characters on *The Winds of Our Tides* be so desperate to reach other characters? Episode after episode, they burst into rooms, careened through towns, and flew across continents in search of other people.

But why did they do all that? *What were people for?* The question felt important. It felt like the most important question ever asked. It felt like—

"You can't go," her mother barked, dragging Leeva back from her thoughts. "Check your Employee Manual." She shot a sharp look at her husband.

For a long moment, Mr. Thornblossom seemed confused. But then he withdrew Leeva's Employee Manual and a pen from the pocket of his recliner. He scribbled in the manual, then held it out. "No going to school. It's right here, under 'Workplace Location Restrictions': No leaving."

Leeva's newly sharpened wits reminded her of something. "But there's an exception for making money or getting famous."

Her mother shook her head so hard her hair-tower snapped. "Yes, but children don't get famous or rich for going to school." She motioned toward the manual. "No school. Read it."

Leeva didn't take the manual—she knew perfectly well what her father had done, and she knew that it was unfair. Whenever she encountered unfairness, it felt as if something in her chest were leaping to its feet, trying to punch its way out. That something was rising up now, but Leeva told it to sit back down.

She needed an idea.

She retreated to her thinking spot in the kitchen.

She'd left the premises exactly twice before, for the two exceptions allowed. Perhaps there was something in one of those occasions that could help her now.

The last time was three or four years ago, when her father had driven her to the Cheap-O Depot Grocery

Warehouse. Leeva had found the store's aisles a wonderland of colors and signs and smells, but her father had hustled her into an office. There, he thrust the *Nutsmore Weekly* at the manager, folded to the Help Wanted ads. "Shelf stocker, night shift," he read aloud. "My daughter will take the job."

"It includes mopping, Mr. Thornblossom," the manager had warned. "Floors get pretty filthy."

"Yeah, fine, she's tough."

"And it's eight p.m. to four a.m. seven nights a week."

"She's not doing anything else then."

"Well, tell her to come in and apply."

"She's right here," Mr. Thornblossom had said.

The manager, sitting at his tall desk, looked right and left, then straight over Leeva's head. "Where?"

Mr. Thornblossom attempted to lift Leeva into the manager's view. Never having held his daughter before, he searched in vain for a handle. Finally, Leeva clambered onto the desk herself. Nights out of her house sounded good to her.

The manager's eyebrows nearly shot off his face. "That's a *child*! There are *laws*!" Then he eyed Leeva more closely, finger to his chin. "She does look strong. Bring her back when she's sixteen."

Leeva had no doubt that her father would do that, but she couldn't wait until she was sixteen.

She thought back to the other occasion she'd been allowed out. It had been even longer ago, but she still remembered.

Her mother had hauled her out of her crib, slapped makeup on her face, shellacked her hair into a fountain, and then wrapped her in sequined netting. Leeva had forgotten all her discomfort when she'd seen the Little Miss and Little Mister Nutsmore Pageant stage. What a dream! Lights, banners, and, best of all, dozens of other tiny girls and boys!

"What's her talent?" asked the host, checking in contestants on a clipboard.

And just like that, the dream came crashing down. Unlike the other contestants, Leeva had never learned a dance step, a note of music, or a line of poetry.

As her mother dragged her off the stage and away from those other children, Leeva's tears had cut deep ravines through her makeup and left her false eyelashes dripping off her chin.

The memory still hurt, but in it, she realized now, was a ray of hope.

Leeva got up and went back into the living room.

"Those Human Inanities," she suggested to her mother at a break in her program. "If I went to school, I could learn them and enter that Little Miss and Little Mister Nutsmore Pageant again. I could win."

"I cancelled that pageant," her mother snapped. She shoved a stack of *Celebrities This Week* at Leeva. "These will teach you about fame."

Her father shoved a stack of *Money Monthly* magazines at her. "These will teach you about money. Stop talking and go away."

Leeva didn't touch the magazines—she'd already seen plenty of them, it was how she'd taught herself to read and do mathematics. And she knew when she was beat, so she did stop talking and she did go away.

Much later, after she'd gotten herself ready for bed and tucked herself in, she lay wide awake thinking about the evening. What came back to her again and again was her father's question.

What are people for?

The question galvanized her already-crackling curiosity. The answer, she felt certain, was out there.

The problem was, she was *in here*.

Well, that would have to change tomorrow.

BEYOND THE HEDGE

The building beside Leeva's house was three stories tall, made of rosy-red brick. From her bedroom window, when the lights were on in this building, she'd often seen people inside. She'd start there.

The instant her parents left the next morning (a Saturday, no matter, her parents worked seven days a week), she bolted out the kitchen door. Leeva had been in the backyard before, of course—it was her job to mow its weeds, page six of the manual, "Workplace Duties." But today, she marched straight to the tall, prickly hedge, the boundary her manual warned she must never cross. Before she could talk herself out of it, she straightened her spine, raised her fists, and crashed in.

The first thing she noticed was the piney, fresh

scent. How had she lived between eight and nine whole years without knowing how thrilling it smelled to push through a boundary? That scent was worth all the scratches. She filled her lungs with it and pushed on through.

Leeva emerged beside a large red metal container, printed with the words *Book Return*. In front of her lay a paved drive.

The drive ran along the side of the rosy-brick building and was painted down its center with instructive yellow arrows.

She stepped out and followed the arrows to the back of the building, where she passed a stoop. Still following the arrows, she rounded another corner. Seeing that the drive only led through a parking lot and then out to the street, Leeva retraced her steps; there'd been a door into the rosy-brick building on that back stoop. She climbed up, walked past pots of herbs, a chair, and a table, and opened that door.

She found herself in a tiny hallway, crowded with boxes, umbrellas, skateboards, gloves, and helmets. Past this clutter, though, was a single spacious, bright room more appealing than any she'd ever seen, even in *The Winds of Our Tides*. Leeva hid behind a huge picture

frame draped in canvas and took it all in for a moment.

Sun streamed through windows whose deep sills were filled with cushions and cheerful scarlet geraniums. Plump chairs and colorful rugs were scattered everywhere. Directly across, double doors stood wide open to the street as if in welcome. Best of all, books and books and books lined every wall and filled tall shelves in the middle of the room.

Leeva had long been curious about books. The people in *The Winds of Our Tides* had lots of them in their homes, and they seemed proud of them, although no one ever did anything with them, except the children, who read them in their beds. And Leeva had often seen books displayed behind the celebrities on her mother's programs. But she'd never seen anything like the abundance in front of her. If she were ever to need her picture taken, this certainly would be the place. That wasn't what she needed today, though.

Leeva stepped out and walked up to the only other person in the place, a sad-faced youngish man seated behind a desk. He was reading one of the books, so apparently grown-ups did that as well. "I have a question," she said.

The sad-faced youngish man straightened up. He

tightened the knot of his tie. "Well, a library is a good place to find answers."

"Library?" asked Leeva, who had never seen the front of the building with its large sign that read Nutsmore Public Library.

"Your first visit?" The sad-faced youngish man—or maybe he was an oldish boy, it can be hard to tell when someone is wearing a tie—closed his book and really looked at Leeva.

Being really looked at was a new experience, and it made Leeva feel more solid somehow. "My first visit," she confirmed.

"Library." He spread his arms. "A place full of books you can read here or take home for a while."

Leeva gasped. "You'd let me read your books?"

"Not *my* books. *Yours.*"

Leeva gasped again. "*My* books?"

"*Your* books. This is a *public* library." He tapped a nameplate. It read *Pauline Flowers*, but *Pauline* had been crossed out and *Harry* had been handwritten over it. "I'm Harry. I'm the librarian here. Well . . . actually, it's only as long as my aunt can't . . ." A look flashed over Harry Flowers's face that was not simple sadness. It was outright misery.

The look barely lasted a second, but Leeva knew it all right. She was an expert in identifying human expressions thanks to her years of studying *The Winds of Our Tides*—soap operas are first-rate training grounds for identifying emotions: Rage, Desire, Shock, Disgust, you name it, portrayed in extreme exaggeration and slow motion, over and over.

"You don't like being a librarian?"

"No, no, I do!" he protested. "Although . . . I'm sorry that I *have* to be one. I mean, I'm happy I can do it, just . . ." Here, he flung himself over the desk, as if he couldn't go on. But then he raised his head and waved toward the nearest armchair. "Oh, I might as well tell you the story."

TEN BOOKS!

Leeva climbed onto the chair. "Your armchair is commodious," she commented. *Commodious—both roomy and comfortable*—was a word she'd learned two years before and had been trying to use since. Using a word was the crowning pleasure of acquiring one, but there had never been anything roomy *or* comfortable in her house.

"Wow, commodious, thanks. So, you see, my aunt is the librarian here. But now she can't get up and down the stairs, not with her knees, not these stairs, anyway."

"What's wrong with her knees?" Leeva asked.

"Cracked, both of them, two months ago. Skateboarding. Just an ollie with a three-sixty, a move she'd done a hundred times, but she hit a pothole." And here he shot a mystifying glare out the window that faced the hedge Leeva had just crashed through.

"Can she get them fixed?"

"She could if . . ." Once more, Harry frowned toward the window. "No, they cut her health insurance. Anyway, the stairs are too unsafe, and she can't fix those either, no money in the budget, so I am filling in for her." He pressed a hand to his heart and raised his voice as if he were addressing the ceiling. "It's an honor to carry on her dream! I ask no more of life than to be allowed to follow in her footsteps!"

It seemed to Leeva that he had practiced this speech before. She swung her feet and listened politely as he explained about carrying on proud heritages and such.

Finally Harry Flowers slumped back in his seat. "So, I'm not a real librarian," he said, "not unless I go to school for it. I guess I'm only the . . . well, the acting librarian."

"*Acting* librarian?"

"Acting! *Yes!*" And suddenly, Harry Flowers didn't look sad. He looked joyful, as if he didn't usually dare hope for something, but for at least this moment he *did* dare hope for it. He sprang out of his seat. "Let me show you around."

The perked-up acting librarian began with a dramatic sweep of his arm. "Here on the first floor is the fiction. Stories." Then he led Leeva up a spiral staircase. The staircase was missing several chunks of railing, some banisters, and a number of treads. Leeva dodged nimbly around the broken parts, which made it more fun.

"Up here are the informational texts," he said when they reached the second floor. "Nonfiction."

The second floor was just as inviting as the first. Leeva wanted to explore it, but Harry took a step down.

Leeva didn't move. She sniffed deeply. "What's that?"

"Oh. Cookies. Oatmeal-apricot today. My aunt and I live on the top floor." He took another step down.

Leeva couldn't move, though. It was as though her nose had hypnotized her legs. She had never smelled anything so wonderful before. "Cookies?"

"It's a life goal of hers—to make every cookie recipe in the world. Now that she can't do her job, it's become even more important."

Just then, there came a splashy crash from above.

Harry nodded as if he'd expected it. "Mixing bowls," he said. "She's washing the dishes." There came another crash—this one more metallic. Harry winced. "There go the spoons."

"It's kind of loud for dishwashing," Leeva noted.

Harry nodded. "Aunt Pauline is pretty unhappy."

"She misses the books," Leeva guessed.

"No, I bring her books," Harry said. "It's matching them up with readers she misses so much. Handing exactly the right book to the right person at the right time and saying, '*This* one.'" Just then came another crash, clinky with broken china. Harry grabbed his temples. "She takes it out on the dishes."

Often, after an especially miserable evening, Leeva found herself knocking pots and pans around in the sink. "I do, too," she said. "It makes you feel better."

The acting librarian gave Leeva a quizzical look and then led her downstairs. There, he settled himself behind his desk. He reached for his book, but then he looked up. "I almost forgot. You had a question."

"Yes. I want to find out: What are people for?"

Harry Flowers reacted with a look full of such complex emotion that even Leeva couldn't read it.

"People? What are they *for*?" he repeated.

"Yes. What is the point of people, please, Harry? What good are they?"

Harry dropped his chin to his hands and studied Leeva hard. He looked so worried that she leaned in and gave him a pat on his shoulder. She'd never given anyone a shoulder pat before, and she'd certainly never received one, but she knew from her soap opera that it was a comforting thing to do.

The pat did it. Harry shook off his worried look. He rubbed his fingers through his hair, which was so tightly curled it looked as if it could spring off his head at any moment. He studied her even harder. Finally he asked, "Can you read?"

Of course, Leeva had taught herself to read years before, and she told him so.

He drew out a chart titled, "Determining Reading Level." "Starting at the top, read the sentences aloud until you get to one you can't."

Leeva did this for a while, but since the sentences were all about someone named Nancy who never did anything interesting at all, she soon grew bored. She picked up the acting librarian's book instead. "'This above all: to thine own self be true,'" she read. "'And it must follow, as the night the day, thou canst not then be false to any man.'"

Harry stared across the desk at her. Leeva recognized his expression as Stunned Happiness. "*Hamlet*, by William Shakespeare," he said. "I guess you can read just fine. How much can you carry?"

"I don't know. I exercise with *Vim and Vigor at Any Age* every day, so I'm pretty strong."

"All right. Say, ten books. Let's go find some. Wait, no," he interrupted himself. His eyes darted up toward the ceiling, and he broke into a smile—small, but real. He held up one finger, as if asking Leeva to stay where she was—which she would have done anyway, she loved this place!—and then he rose from his desk, spiraled up the staircase to the third floor, and disappeared.

Leeva heard a faint murmuring of voices, then a few moments later, Harry came back down holding a sheet of paper. He circled the library, consulting the paper and picking books off the shelves.

He returned and stacked the books into her arms. "My aunt feels these will give you a good start on learning what people are for. Read them, then come back and we'll give you ten more."

Leeva couldn't

believe her luck. Ten books, all for her! She hurried for the door. But just as she got there, Harry called, "Wait."

Leeva pulled the books closer to her chest. Reader, now that she had them, she wasn't going to give them up easily.

"Come back," he repeated. "But from now on, come in the afternoons. We open back up at one o'clock each day."

GETTA GRIPPE?

Leeva read all ten books, then returned to the library the next afternoon and got ten more. She did this every day for a week, because once she'd discovered the miraculous world next door, that hedge wasn't going to keep her from it anymore, no sirree. To keep her outings a secret, Leeva always broke through at the same spot and fluffed the branches back in place, just in case her parents ever prowled the backyard.

But wait. Let's back up, Reader.

When Leeva walked in that second afternoon, Harry Flowers said, "I'm awfully sorry. I was supposed to get you a library card yesterday." He pulled out a pen and an important-looking yellow card. "Now, first name?"

When Leeva told him, he said, "Oh! That's a great

name. And I bet it has a great story to go along with it."

Leeva looked down at the floor. "No. It doesn't."

Apparently, when Leeva was born, it had come as a nasty shock to Mrs. Thornblossom that she had to put any effort at all into the business of being a mother.

The maternity nurse, Nurse Blackberry, who was a very patient woman actually, had had it with the mayor's constant demands—*Do this! Fetch me that!*—all day long. She was fed up, ready to snap. And now here she was, holding the birth certificate, asking what the new baby's name was and hearing in reply, "Don't you know who I am? You do it, nurse!"

Well, Nurse Blackberry snapped. "Look! The last name is filled in already: Thornblossom! All that's left is . . ." She rapped her pointer finger sharply on the empty line. "First and middle names."

Mrs. Thornblossom kicked her stilettos against the sheets and flopped onto her pillow. "I'm famous. You do it!" she ordered again.

Nurse Blackberry would not. She was truly at the end of her patience. She stabbed the document harder. "First name. Middle name," she read through gritted teeth. "Leave a space."

"There. That wasn't so hard, was it?" muttered Mayor

Thornblossom. "Write it in." She snapped on her satin eye mask, rolled over, and began to snore.

It took the nurse a moment to realize what had just happened: She'd been told to name this darling baby *Leave a Space*. And the horrid mother had rolled over and gone to sleep!

Well, Nurse Blackberry did the best she could under the circumstances: She spelled it in an attractive manner.

Each time her parents related the story, they cackled in glee. But Leeva knew it wasn't funny. In fact, it was a pitiful thing to have been named so carelessly. But as a positive person, she consoled herself that it could have been worse. What if Nurse Blackberry had yelled "Get a grip!" or "Print neatly!" or "You're driving me bonkers!" instead? How about those for names? Clearly it could have been much worse.

Still, Leeva didn't want to tell the story to anyone, and certainly not to the very nice, but sad-faced, acting librarian. "Leeva," she repeated, spelling it. "Leeva Spayce—"

Just then came another crash from above, this one accompanied by a growling so loud it could probably be heard on the street.

Harry dropped the pen and sprinted up the broken stairs.

When he returned, he was frowning. "Unbelievable," he muttered, taking his seat. "No money for the library for three years, but plenty for a statue . . ."

"Oh, you know about Mayor Thornblossom's stat—"

"Stop!" Harry swept a warning finger to his lips and pointed up. "Don't ever let my aunt *hear* that name. Those Thornblossoms are . . . Well, never mind. It doesn't involve you." Harry picked up the important-looking card. "Now, Leeva . . . what was it? Space?"

Leeva gulped. "S-P-A-Y-C-E," she spelled. She pressed her lips together firmly against her forbidden last name.

"Well, Leeva Spayce, this card means you are trusted to take out books and return them unharmed." Harry held it out.

Leeva's hands trembled as she reached to take it. A card of trust! Reverently, she slipped it into the pocket of her T-shirt, as close to her heart as possible.

The library card was a treasure, of course. But there was another gift that day.

"Oh, I almost forgot: the reason I wanted you to come back in the afternoon." Harry sprinted up the

spiral staircase again and a minute later came back down. He handed Leeva a small bundle wrapped in a blue-and-white cloth napkin.

Leeva peeled up a corner. Inside were three plump, crumbly cookies that smelled delicious.

"From Aunt Pauline. Chocolate chunk with toasted hazelnuts today." Harry stacked ten new books into Leeva's arms, balanced the cookies on top, and Leeva went back to her house and ate the cookies slowly and read the books quickly.

Each afternoon for the rest of the week she returned.

Sometimes there were other people in the library. Leeva greeted them *Hello* and they greeted her *Hello* back, which made her feel as if they were on the same team, the team of people who visited this library.

Sometimes the library was empty, which was nice, too, because then Harry wasn't always dashing up to the nonfiction floor for people who couldn't use the stairs. Leeva liked having Harry all to herself. Harry really listened to her, which was a new experience. Instead of telling her to stop talking and go away, his whole being seemed to invite her to keep talking and stay awhile.

Either way, she brought back her ten books every day and Harry replaced them with ten more his aunt suggested.

Each afternoon, Leeva also brought back the empty napkin, neatly folded. And each afternoon she received three more delicious cookies.

By the way, Reader, there had not once been so much as a cookie crumb at the Thornblossom home. Apparently celebrities never ate cookies, or if they did, they didn't tell *Celebrities This Week* magazine about it.

Nor were cookies ever on the Rock-Bottom Sale shelf at Cheap-O Depot Grocery Warehouse. So you can imagine how those cookies brightened Leeva's life.

More importantly, ten books for seven days is seventy books. And books, Leeva found out, did a whole lot more than merely look good as backgrounds in photographs. Reader, here are some of her favorites:

New Kid; *Charlotte's Web*; *Where the Mountain Meets the Moon*; *Bud, Not Buddy*; *Other Words for Home*; *One Crazy Summer*; *Because of Winn-Dixie*.

(Reader, that last one also shows the incredible, courageous, somber, hilarious, steadfast value of dogs, and after she read it, Leeva resolved to read seventy books about *that* someday.)

Ten books and three cookies each day. After a week like that, Leeva felt ready.

THE PUNISHMENT

"I want to go to school and be with people," Leeva plunged in after dinner. "People are not just for getting money from and being famous to. People are for helping you find your dog who's afraid of lightning, and for eating pickles with. They are for saving your life if you are going to be killed just because you're a runt. For pretending to be the family of a hungry runaway boy so he can get a meal. People keep you from feeling lonely or scared or—"

"Where did you get that malarkey?" her mother asked.

"I read seventy books. The people in those books—"

"Books? People in books don't have money!" her father laughed. He tapped the side of his head, as if he was about to impart something very wise. "So they aren't real. They are just printed words on paper."

Leeva realized that her father was both right and wrong. He was right that if you opened up a book, you would see printed words. Not real people. But he was also wrong. Because now Leeva knew that as you read a book, those words *became* real people, doing real things. By the end of a book, those words left you weeping or cheering or vowing to change your life.

Words had true power, Leeva realized. No wonder she searched the *Nutsmore Weekly* each Friday to learn a new one.

Before she could pursue this revelation, her mother snapped off her television. She got up. She began to pace. *Clink-clink-clink.* "Where did you get those seventy books?" she demanded, stopping in front of Leeva. "Certainly not in this house."

Leeva gulped. Then she straightened up. Her parents lied, but she wouldn't. "At the library. Next door."

Her father looked up from his show. "Did you get any money there?"

"Money? Um . . . it's a library. They lend you books."

Mayor Thornblossom ducked to her mirror. She gave herself a wink. "Am I famous in there?"

"Famous? It's a library," Leeva repeated. "Some of the books are famous, I think."

Leeva's father seemed to lose interest then. But her mother frowned and began to grind her heel. "Didn't you talk about me in there?"

"I never said your name," Leeva admitted truthfully. "I can't."

Her mother's eyes widened. Then they narrowed dangerously. "Is that so?" She loomed over Leeva, *scritch-scritch-SCRITCH*. "Well, then, you're not to go into that library again."

Leeva gasped. The something that lived in her chest, the thing that hated unfairness, raised its fists. But she remembered just in time: She had to be on guard now, more cautious. The *scritch*ing was getting sharper, a clear warning sign. If handing out punishments were a sport, her mother would have a neckful of gold medals, and she was just getting warmed up. Who knew what she might do next?

Leeva told the thing in her chest to settle down for now, fold its hands on its lap.

Two new programs began on her parents' sets. "Stop talking and go away," Leeva's mother said.

And Leeva did.

She ran up to her room and flung herself on her bed. *I should run away*, she thought bitterly. Lots of kids in the books she'd read this last week had run away. It made their families sorry, all right. It taught them a lesson.

Leeva rolled over. Who was she kidding? The kids in those books were brave enough to strike out alone. Was she?

And even if she were brave enough to run away, where would she go?

COOKIE BUCKET

The next morning, for the first time ever, Leeva went back to bed after her parents left for work. She was feeling sorry for herself, and bed is an excellent location for that.

But around the middle of the day, when she couldn't bear to look at the cracks in her ceiling any longer, she pulled her stack of library books out from under the bed.

It had become clear over the past week that the lives of the characters in the books she'd read had little in common with her own. None of them, for example, checked their Employee Manuals for what they must and must not do. Come to think of it, none of them even seemed to *have* Employee Manuals.

Leeva had finished *A Wrinkle in Time* at midnight.

Its heroine, Meg, had endured many trials trying to rescue the people she loved. She had bravely crossed galaxies—no hedge boundaries for her!—and traveled through time; she had faced an evil disembodied brain. Through it all, she'd never given up.

Friday's vocabulary word had been *Persist—to continue firmly in a course of action in spite of difficulty, opposition, or failure.* The way Meg had persisted inspired Leeva now.

She got out of bed. She crossed to her window. She rested her cheek on the glass and reached into her pajama top to stroke her library card, which she wore in a little plastic bag tied with twine around her neck so it would be close to her heart.

The card trusted her to bring back her books, and so she would do that today, along with her cookie napkin. But today, and from now on, she could not go inside.

No more greetings. No more books. No more cookies. No more Harry Flowers.

Thinking about this made her arms and legs feel too heavy to move. She could barely lift her head off her chest.

Nevertheless, she persisted.

She washed her face. She brushed her teeth. She

dressed. She went outside, pushed through the hedge, and placed the books and the napkin on the table on the back stoop. And then she knocked on the door. Even her knuckles felt heavy.

"Come on in, Leeva," Harry called.

Hearing his voice made Leeva's throat tighten. She had to fight to hold back her tears. She opened the door a crack. "I can't," she sniffed. "Not anymore."

When Harry came out, she told him the news. "My mother won't let me. It's a punishment."

"Forbidding you to come into the library is a punishment? That seems awfully unfair." Harry looked even sadder than usual.

Leeva picked up the napkin and wiped her eyes. And doing this, she realized something important: Although nothing in her situation had changed, she *felt* better. While she'd read in many of the seventy books that sharing sadness was one of the things that people were for, she'd just experienced it herself.

And then, with her newly sharpened wits, she realized something else. Something quite astonishing: Yes, her mother had forbidden her to step inside the library, but she hadn't said a word about her leaving the yard. In their disappointment at not becoming richer or more famous, her parents had missed Leeva's bigger offense!

"Maybe, Harry," Leeva said, brightening a little, "maybe we could visit out here sometimes?"

Harry nodded. "How about this? The library is closed between noon and one every afternoon. You come here at that time, and we'll have lunch together. And then I'll bring some new books out, and it will be almost the same."

Leeva held up the napkin. "Also the cookies?"

"Sure, also the cookies."

"Could we start today?"

Harry checked his watch. "I'll go up and make lunch."

He left and returned a few moments later with a tray of food: two egg salad sandwiches with tiny sweet pickles on the side, two plump plums, and a jug of lemonade with two cups. He shared it all with Leeva. It was the most delicious meal she had ever eaten. Sitting on the sun-warmed boards of the stoop, Leeva felt as if she were being warmed too, but from Harry's kindness.

Just then, a third-floor window creaked open. A woman popped her head out.

Harry pointed up. "That's my aunt." He motioned toward Leeva. "Aunt Pauline, this is the girl I've been

telling you about."

Leeva squinted up. Pauline Flowers wore a scarf that fluttered in the breeze and earrings that flashed silver in the sun. Purple hair crowned her head and her glasses were pink as flamingos.

Leeva cupped her hands to her mouth. "Thank you for all the cookies," she called up. "They are the best things I have ever tasted. They are . . ." She searched for a word up to the task. *"Deluxe!"* she finished.

"Harry told me you can't come inside." She held up a just-one-minute finger. She ducked away, but quickly reappeared with a tin bucket. She lowered the bucket on a rope until Leeva could reach it. Inside was a bundle of still-warm cookies.

Leeva took it out, tucked yesterday's napkin in the bucket, and bowed as Mrs. Flowers hauled it up. "And thank you for the books. They are . . ." Even after years of learning new words, Leeva couldn't express how much the books had meant to her.

Mrs. Flowers seemed to understand. She crossed her hands over her heart. "Were they the right ones? Were they what you needed?" she called down, looking hopeful.

"Exactly the right ones," Leeva assured her.

For an instant, Leeva saw a look of satisfaction shine on the librarian's face. But then she heard the growl she'd heard in the library often during the past week. "The fact that I can't do it myself just infuriates me," she heard.

"I'm sorry about your cracked knees," Leeva offered.

"Me, too, believe me. But it's not only me, you know. Lots of our patrons can't navigate those stairs. What really upsets me is that Harry has to take over. Just for the summer, though, I will not allow it any longer. Then he's off to London. The Royal Shakespeare Acting School, Leeva! He was accepted for the fall. I'm so proud! Did he tell you?"

Leeva looked at Harry.

Harry nodded, then turned away.

"He should be there now, actually," Mrs. Flowers went on. "Just a few weeks more and you're off, Harry!"

"The library opens soon, Aunt Pauline," he shouted up. "Better make Leeva's list."

"All right. What are you in the mood for today,

Leeva? Funny or serious?"

That was hard. "Some of both," Leeva decided.

"The setting: Here or far away?"

That was easier. "As far away as possible, please."

"I know just the books." Mrs. Flowers disappeared.

"She's her old self again," Harry said. "At least when she's choosing titles for you each day. She misses working terribly. But I'm going to fix it."

"How, Harry?" Leeva asked.

Mrs. Flowers came back then and let fly a paper airplane.

Harry put his finger to his lips, plucked the paper from a pot of basil, and then hurried inside without answering Leeva.

LEEVA SETS OUT

The next day was a special one—the third Monday of the month. It was special because on the third Monday of every month, the Cheap-O Depot Grocery Warehouse gave an extra 5 percent off to senior citizens. On that day, Mr. Thornblossom powdered his mustache, bent over a cane, and shuffled into the store to claim the discount on fifty Cheezaroni blocks.

His disguise fooled precisely no one, Reader. "Here comes that cheater-pants Thornblossom," the clerks all muttered when they heard him tapping his cane at the door. But did anyone call him on his deceit? No, they did not. Because if they did, *bam!* They would be slapped with an extra tax quicker than you could say Cheezaroni.

All morning, Leeva was anxious, hoping her father's

return wouldn't interfere with her library visit. And she was in luck—at just past eleven she heard the car. A few minutes later, her father struggled in, laden with bags. He dumped them on the counter with a groan, swiped the powder from his mustache, then removed one package from the bag and peeled it open—it was his special treat to eat one brick raw the day he stocked up, when it was the freshest. He took a big bite. "Cook the rest of these up," he mumbled through the orange mush. "I'm going back to work."

Leeva made short work of the cooking and plunged into the hedge at 11:59.

After checking, as she always did, to make sure Harry wasn't at the window—if he saw her coming from her yard and asked about it, how could she avoid saying her forbidden name?—she wriggled out and hurried to the library's back stoop. She placed her books, her napkin, and the Cheezaroni block she'd brought for lunch on the table.

Just as the Town Hall clock struck twelve, Harry came outside. He loosened his tie and unbuttoned the top of his shirt. Then he picked up the heavy orange food brick, grimacing as he caught a whiff, and propped open the door with it. "Good idea. Now I can hear if the phone rings." He looked at the table, then at Leeva's empty hands. "Nothing for lunch?"

Leeva eyed the Cheezaroni block. "No, nothing," she said.

Just then, Leeva heard a car approach, then stop, its engine idling. She peered around the corner. A gray car had pulled up at the big red metal box.

"Just someone returning books," Harry told her.

The car started up again. Harry waved as it passed by the stoop. "I usually collect them in the morning, but come on, Leeva, I'll show you how it works."

Leeva followed Harry to the book drop and watched closely as he pressed some numbers into the keypad and opened the big door at the bottom. Inside were a few books tumbled onto a folded quilt. Harry scooped them out and walked them into the library. When he came back out, he brought lunch, which he shared again: tuna fish and frilly lettuce on soft buns, carrot sticks, and a bunch of purple grapes.

As she ate, Leeva kept glancing up at the open window on the third floor.

"She's still baking," Harry said, noticing. "Which reminds me of something I forgot yesterday. Each day on my break, I run out for the ingredients she'll need for the next day's recipe."

Just then came a slamming crash from inside. Harry grimaced. "The oven door. Aunt Pauline is *extra cranky* today. Something about a new tax—"

Mrs. Flowers leaned out the window then, waving a spatula. "Cranky? *Cranky?!*"

Harry leaped up. "I only meant—"

"If I find ants in the sugar bowl, you'll see me cranky. If you knock over that oregano plant again, I'll show you cranky, all right!"

Harry stepped swiftly away from the potted herbs and Leeva put down her sandwich. Something more interesting than tuna fish was going on upstairs.

"Do not tell that child I am cranky. I am *way* beyond that. I am *infuriated*. I am *seething with rage*. I am *on fire with righteous indignation!*"

"Sorry, Aunt Pauline, I only—"

"And not only that, I'll have you both know that I am *good at it!*" With that, the window slammed shut.

Harry sat back down. He looked mortified. "Don't worry. She's all bark."

"Oh, no, I'm not worried," Leeva assured him. "I really liked it."

Harry gave her a strange look. "You *liked* it?"

"A lot. Especially that last thing. On fire with . . . ?"

"Oh. Righteous indignation."

"Definition, please?"

"Well, indignation is a kind of outrage, and the righteous part means the outrage is about something unfair."

Leeva began to crackle with excitement. "Does it feel as if something is standing up in your chest and waving its fists?"

"Uh-huh. Exactly."

Leeva picked up her sandwich again, mightily pleased. She had the words for it now.

"Anyway, I have to go out for whatever special ingredient Aunt Pauline will need for her baking the next day," Harry said. "So, I'm sorry, but I can't spend the whole hour with you."

The last bite of sandwich clogged in Leeva's throat. She swallowed. "Could you go at night, after the library closes?"

"No, not at night. I got a part in a play at the Community Theater. We rehearse in the evenings."

Leeva was about to argue that maybe he could give up a *little bit* of his rehearsal time, but then she saw his face. You didn't need to study soap operas to read his expression as Determined Passion. "What is it you love so much about acting?"

Harry squinted in thought for a moment. "The stories, of course. But it's the chance to try on other people's lives I like the best. To walk someone else's path."

Harry's words triggered an idea. "Harry! You don't have to go get the ingredients anymore."

He raised a hand. "Oh, I do. She's stuck up there, can't do her job . . . At least I can make sure she has that."

"No. I mean, *you* don't have to. *Someone else* can walk that path. *Me*, Harry!" Leeva cried. "Every day, you tell me what she needs and where to get it, and *I'll* do it!"

Harry munched a handful of grapes, frowning and then nodding, frowning and nodding. "Are you sure?" he said at last. "You'd be encountering a lot of people, Leeva. And they won't all be . . . Well, let's say they'll be a mix. Are you ready for that?"

Leeva sat up taller. What better way could there be for learning what people are for than encountering a mix of them? "I am definitely ready for that."

"All right, then." Harry got up and went inside. When he came back, he sat beside her and unfolded a map across his knees. "So here we are in Nutsmore." He tapped the middle of the map. "The library, on Almond

Avenue." Then he handed Leeva a slip of paper. On it was written: *one half cup sesame seeds*. Below that was an address: *115 Filbert Street*.

"Will I need money to buy them?" Leeva asked.

Harry shook his head. "Folks donate the ingredients." He helped Leeva locate the address on the map and plot the best route. "I'll meet you back here at five fifteen for those sesame seeds," he promised. Then, when the Town Hall clock struck one, he buttoned his shirt, tightened his tie, and went back inside.

And Leeva, full of the pride of knowing she was helping someone achieve her life's goal, also full of tuna fish and grapes, set out.

LIFE-THREATENING BRAIDS

Her destination was five blocks away, and Leeva enjoyed every one of them. All around her, birds sang, trees reached their leafy arms into the blue sky, and flowers waved their sweet-smelling blooms as if greeting her. The outside world was fresher and crisper and brighter than she'd expected. In fact, the outside world seemed as delightful as one of the laxative ads that peppered Leeva's soap opera.

But what really engaged Leeva were the swing sets, tree houses, Popsicle sticks, and gum wrappers that hinted at children nearby. If she weren't on such an important mission, she would follow these clues and find those kids. But in just a few minutes she reached her destination—a sturdy stone house next to a park.

Leeva was surprised to see that the address was lettered plainly on a mailbox beside the front door. Even odder, there were no doorway briars—it was as if the people who lived here weren't even trying to deter visitors!

Above the door was a sign: FRISK INSURANCE— Life Is Risky, Insure with Frisky.

Leeva knocked.

"Come in! Watch your step!" two cheery voices called.

Inside, a man and a woman sat at desks facing each other. Both of them spun around in swivel chairs when Leeva entered.

"You look like someone who needs an insurance policy!" the woman cried, her cheeks stretched alarmingly wide.

"No, actually," Leeva began, "I—"

The man stabbed a finger at Leeva. "Have you considered what would happen in the unfortunate event of your demise?"

Leeva knew that "the unfortunate event of her demise" meant her death, and she was startled that it was the subject of these people's conversation. "No, I have not considered that," she admitted truthfully.

Mr. and Mrs. Frisk jumped out from behind their desks. "Life is full of dangers at your age. We have a son, ten years old, so we should know," said Mrs. Frisk, taking a step toward Leeva. "Crocodiles, avalanches, rolling out of bed—"

"Blowfish livers, sword-swallowing, murder hornets," Mr. Frisk warned, advancing as well.

"Your braids alone—they're a multiple hazard. They could strangle you, trip you, you could swallow them in your sleep!" Mrs. Frisk ticked off the hair-based perils on her fingers.

Leeva clutched her braids. Both Mr. and Mrs. Frisk seemed deeply concerned with her welfare, and this was a refreshing change from the way her own parents treated her. But Leeva also felt cornered. She edged back toward the door.

"The point is," Mr. Frisk urged darkly, "how would your family get along without your contributions?"

This question stopped Leeva in her tracks. For the past week, she had been wondering, *What were people for?* and now here these two Frisks were, asking, basically, *What was* she *for?*

What good was she, anyway?

Her parents complained often that she hadn't

brought them any more money or fame, and suddenly Leeva felt a twinge of guilt about this. It was difficult to think how she could have accomplished it without being allowed off the premises, but now that she was out, she would try to do better. Maybe, if she became the daughter they wanted, they'd become the parents she wanted.

Right now, though, she desperately wanted to report to the Frisks that she contributed *something*.

She thought hard. She spent a lot of time in the kitchen, of course, most of it washing dishes. Leeva closed her eyes and imagined what would happen if she stopped. "In the unfortunate event of my demise," she concluded finally, "my parents would probably start using paper plates."

As soon as she said it, she saw that her demise wouldn't be much of an unfortunate event for them at all. Even adding in all her other chores, she really wouldn't be missed.

But then one thing occurred to her. "I am useful to my father! I solve bookkeeping problems for him." She'd never asked why he needed those problems solved. All she knew was that he insisted she sign each page and that the work had involved larger figures lately. She was wearing down pencils at a remarkable clip. "He can't do them without me."

"We have just the policy." Mrs. Frisk scooped up a sheaf of papers and brandished them. "For a mere twenty-seven ninety-nine a month, you can have peace of mind. Less than a dollar a day. Quite a bargain, don't you agree?"

Leeva certainly did agree that $27.99 was a bargain for peace of mind—who wouldn't?—although she didn't understand how a stack of paper could bring it. But she had to admit that she didn't have any money. "I'm only here to ask for some sesame seeds."

At this news, both Frisks slumped back behind their desks. "Nice to meet you," they mumbled, heads down, "go around back, find Osmund, he'll get you those seeds, don't choke on them, goodbye."

BOY IN A
HAZMAT SUIT

Leeva walked around back. As she raised her knuckles to knock, she heard the *snap, snap, snap* of three locks unlocking. The door opened the few cautious inches allowed by a chain.

Inside stood a boy—well, she assumed it was a boy, since the Frisks had mentioned a son—dressed hood-to-booties in a yellow paper suit. He crossed his arms over his chest and glared out warily.

Leeva suddenly realized something embarrassing: She had forgotten to prepare for this moment! Quickly, she reviewed the doorstep greetings she'd witnessed on *The Winds of Our Tides*. After "Hello!" the characters always summarized what had happened on the previous episode, which was no help to Leeva now, since she'd never *had* a previous episode with this suspicious, paper-suited Osmund boy.

The only strategy she could come up with for this new situation was to behave as she would want someone else to behave toward her. "My name is Leeva and I am on a mission of utmost importance," she began.

The boy shot a *Halt* palm through the door opening.

He was, Leeva decided, the human equivalent to doorway briars. But she was not deterred. "Pauline Flowers, the librarian, needs half a cup of sesame seeds. Her nephew says you'll give it to me."

"Harry is asking? Oh." Osmund pulled back his hand. He unchained the door. "Well, okay, then." He led Leeva into his kitchen, where he hurried over to a table. Spread over one end of the table was an assortment of figurines. Before Leeva could see any more, he threw a tablecloth over the whole array.

Osmund donned safety glasses and snapped on some gloves. Then he sat at the bare end of the table and began to pour tiny white seeds from a jar into a measuring cup.

While he did this, Leeva regarded his outfit more closely. It zipped up the front and was snugged with elastic around the face and wrists. "What are you wearing?" she asked, making sure to use an admiring tone, the way a visitor on *The Winds of Our Tides* might ask a host about a new hat or a snazzy scarf.

"Hazmat suit." Osmund raised the measuring cup to his eye level and squinted.

"Hazmat?"

"Hazardous materials. The suit protects me from them." He began removing seeds from the measuring cup with a pair of tweezers and dropping them back into the jar.

Leeva looked around. It seemed like a perfectly harmless kitchen. "Are there hazardous materials here?"

The boy gave her an incredulous look. "They're everywhere!" he cried, waving the tweezers about. "*Life* is a hazardous material!" He shook his head, then bent to his task again.

Life was a hazardous material? Leeva was disturbed, but also intrigued. "So you wear that suit all the time?"

"Of course not," he scoffed, as if the idea were ridiculous. "It's a Level D." He poured the seeds into an envelope and sealed it up, then he thumped the empty measuring cup down with enough force that Leeva understood her visit was over.

Life is a hazardous material!

But at the thump, a small furred animal skittered out from under the table. It had beady black eyes, a striped forehead, and a tail that looked as if someone had forgotten to finish the job.

Osmund jumped up and shooed the animal back under the table. He pocketed the envelope of seeds and eyed Leeva sharply. "You did not see that."

Leeva squared her shoulders and eyed him back just as sharply. She was getting those sesame seeds. "I did see that. What is it, anyway?" she asked. "A skunk? An opossum? Raccoon?"

Osmund met each guess with disdain. "Bob is a badger."

Badgers had never been mentioned in either of her parents' magazines, and they were not well represented on *The Winds of Our Tides*. "I don't know anything about them," Leeva admitted.

"They're dangerous. Rabies, bovine tuberculosis, fleas. That's all you need to know."

Leeva was unimpressed. Hadn't she just found out she'd survived an exhaustive list of dangers already? Besides, this creature was barely the size of her hand. She couldn't suppress a tiny "Ha!" of derision.

"Nothing is funny here!" Osmund shouted. "My parents already killed his parents, and if they find him, they'll kill him, too. My parents are murderers!"

Just then, as if he'd called them, the murderers burst in, waving documents.

"You could pay over time," Mr. Frisk crowed at Leeva.

"Sign right here for that peace of mind!" Mrs. Frisk slapped the documents onto the table.

At the slap, Bob jumped out again.

For five long seconds, everyone froze.

Then all at once: Bob sneezed, Osmund scooped the little badger to his chest, and his parents went flying outside screaming, "Get the hatchet! Get the hatchet!"

Osmund grabbed a backpack from a closet and shoved Bob inside. He thrust the pack at Leeva. "You have to take him for me, keep him safe."

"I can't."

"You have to, right now. Or else . . ."

"Or else, what?"

"Or else . . . I won't give you these seeds."

"Why don't you just let him go?"

"Because he doesn't have a home anymore." Osmund cradled the backpack closer. "Those Thornblossoms!"

Leeva felt the blood drain from her face. "What did they do, those Thornblossoms?"

"Mayor Thornblossom! The garden in the park a block over, where Bob lived—she had it torn up to make room for her statue. Bob's family escaped into our yard, but my parents caught his parents and . . ." Osmund made a disturbing gesture across his throat. "I hid Bob just in time."

Bob poked his head out of the backpack and looked accusingly at Leeva. *None of this murderous tragedy would have happened if it weren't for your mother!* the look said.

Leeva gulped. "All right," she said. "I'll take him."

Osmund secured the backpack on Leeva's shoulders and gave her a shove toward the door.

Leeva braced her feet and held out a hand. "First, the seeds."

Leeva shredded newspapers to make a nest under the kitchen sink. "My parents won't find you here," she assured Bob. "They never come into the kitchen."

This was true. Mostly.

Mrs. Thornblossom had all her celebrity food delivered, and it was Leeva who brought it in from the doorstep. Her mother would probably need a map to find her way to the sink.

Her father did enter the kitchen, but only once a month for that Cheezaroni sale, which had happened just this morning.

Bob would be perfectly safe here.

While the badger explored his new home, Leeva explored the backpack. Each Cleverton twin had one, so she was familiar with the main idea. But she hadn't expected the encouraging way it straightened her shoulders as she'd walked this afternoon; the way it gave her a sense of purpose. The way it seemed to say to her, like the trainers on *Vim and Vigor*, "You can do it!"

And now, looking at it closely, she was delighted to find that not only was the main compartment securely zippered, but tucked inside and out were several more zippered pouches of differing sizes. The intrigue, the promise! The things she could store in here, safe and unseen!

Leeva scolded herself back to reality. She didn't own anything to go in these pouches, did she? Besides, the pack wasn't hers, it was Osmund's.

Then again, he'd put it on her shoulders as if she'd deserved it, and so maybe, at least as long as she had Bob, maybe she did.

HARRY'S SECRET

When Harry emerged at 5:15, he looked entirely different. His tie was gone, he wore red running shoes, and his dress shirt flapped open over a bright T-shirt and jeans.

"You look . . . *Harry-er!*" As she said it, she realized it wasn't just his clothes. He didn't look sad anymore. And she could see now he was an oldish boy, not a youngish man. Definitely.

"Thanks," he said with a grin. "I *feel* Harry-er! Now, how'd your adventure go?"

"Getting sesame seeds was an adventure?"

"Sure. You can't predict what's going to happen when you set off for somewhere new."

Leeva handed him the seeds and told him about

Osmund, and about his parents who cared so much about her safety. She did not mention Bob, or the fact that the badger was orphaned and homeless because of her own mother.

Harry slid the envelope into his pocket and pointed to the table. "Well, your books and your cookies. See you tomorrow." And then he waved and started for the street.

Leeva suddenly felt empty. "Do you have to go right now?"

Harry turned. "Rehearsal starts at six," he said, walking backward. "I like to get there a little early to sit in the park for a few minutes beforehand. It helps me to center myself, before going from Harry-the-librarian to Harry-the-actor."

Leeva felt her shoulders sink.

Harry seemed to notice. He stopped. "Want to walk with me?"

Leeva glanced toward her house. Her parents wouldn't be back for an hour. She ran to catch up.

Before she knew it, they had passed Osmund's house and were at a big, green open space.

"Nutsmore Public Park," Harry said, perching on the back of an empty bench. "These days, the lawns need mowing and the gardens need weeding, but it's nice, right?"

Leeva looked around. She didn't care about mown lawns and weeded gardens; the park was lovely. All except for an ugly bare patch right in the center.

This was the place, Leeva realized. The place where Bob and his family had lived happily until her mother had ordered it scraped. Leeva turned away, looking instead at the people in the park. There were dozens of them, all sizes and ages and colors and shapes, sitting alone or walking in pairs or playing in groups.

Leeva lifted her gaze. Shops lined three sides of the square, many of them hung with Closed or Going Out

of Business signs. On the fourth side were larger stone buildings. Community Theater, read the sign on one. Nutsmore Savings Bank, read another. Town Hall, read the one in the center.

Leeva froze. Her parents were in that Town Hall.

Then she noticed that iron bars crisscrossed the windows and the glass had been newspapered over. Her parents, she remembered, had complained about people trying to peep in.

Relieved that she couldn't be seen, Leeva climbed onto the bench and balanced herself on its back. It wasn't as comfortable as the seat would be, but it made her feel vimful and vigorous to perch there. It made her feel part of a club with Harry. She would have been perfectly content just taking in the scene next to him, but she wanted something else even more. "Are you centered enough yet?" she asked politely.

"Am I . . . ? Oh. Oh, sure. What's on your mind?"

"I just want to keep talking with you. What's the play you're in?"

"*Our Town*, by Thornton Wilder. It's a classic. It's about . . . well . . . this." Harry spread his arms. "An average day in a small town. And how you can see what's most important in life through what ordinary people do.

The things that happen everywhere, every day, the universal things are all in it."

Leeva relaxed as she sat there listening to Harry, who seemed so happy waiting to become Harry-the-actor. His happiness made Leeva feel happy, too. She made a mental note: People were for sharing happiness with, too.

He turned to her. "You know, there's a part for a young girl that hasn't been cast yet . . ."

"Oh, no. I can't."

Harry's eyes crinkled kindly. "Lots of people are afraid of going on stage. Stage fright. I know a trick for that. And you might be a good actress. How will you know if you don't try?"

"It's not that." Suddenly, Leeva didn't want to tell Harry about serving her parents dinner and washing the dishes and scrubbing the floor. She didn't want him to know that she'd never be able to come out at night. "Yesterday, you said you were going to fix something," she said instead. "About your aunt and how she misses work."

"Right!" Harry leaned back and crossed his arms behind his head. "Aunt Pauline doesn't know yet, but I've bought an elevator for the library! It'll be here next week."

"Oh, she'll be so happy! So she can be a librarian again, and you can go to that school in London."

Harry dropped his arms. "Well . . . actually . . . no. See, I used the money I'd saved for school to buy the elevator, so I won't be going."

"Oh, no, Harry! But then . . . how could she be happy if you make yourself so sad?"

"It will be worth it. Aunt Pauline will have her job back."

Harry said it firmly, but Leeva wasn't convinced. In fact, now that she knew people shared each other's happiness and sadness, she was pretty sure Harry's idea was a bad one.

"She raised me," Harry was going on. "I owe her everything, so I do everything I can for her. Like with her life goal . . ." He patted his pocket. "I make sure she has what she needs."

This reminded Leeva of a question she had. "How does she make cookies with just half a cup of sesame seeds?"

"Oh, she keeps plenty of the cookie basics around—butter, sugar, and flour," Harry said. "But each recipe needs different ingredients, and you wouldn't believe how many recipes there are. They're endless."

Leeva, who was knowledgeable in mathematical

theory, had to correct him. "Unless there's an infinite number of ingredients, there can't actually be an endless number of recipes."

"I guess not. Almost, though. First of all, there are a hundred and ninety-five countries in the world, and most of them have some sort of cookies. Then within each major cookie group, there are the variations. Take gingersnaps. You think *gingersnaps, one cookie*, right?"

Leeva nodded, not because she did think *gingersnaps, one cookie*, but because she was in a daze of general agreement.

Harry snapped his fingers. "But *nope*! There are Crispy Gingersnaps, Chewy—"

"Excuse me," Leeva interrupted. "*Nope?*"

"You don't know 'nope'? It means no, but with more . . . oh, oomph. More pizzazz."

"Huh. Oomph. Pizzazz."

"And 'yep' is yes with more oomph, more pizzazz. Same thing. Now, as I was saying, you've got Crispy Gingersnaps, Chewy Gingersnaps, and Crunchy Gingersnaps. You've got Double-Ginger Gingersnaps and Triple-Ginger Gingersnaps. Old-Fashioned

Gingersnaps and New-Fashioned Gingersnaps. There's a week right there. And those are just the gingersnaps in this country. You see?"

"I do," Leeva said. "I see about other countries having different kinds of cookies. And I understand about major cookie groups and multiplying by the variations. But Harry?"

Harry raised his eyebrows.

"What's a gingersnap?"

THE ACTRESS

Leeva was dismayed to find the cupboard floor all gouged up, as if Bob had been trying to escape. "No, no," she soothed, pulling him into her lap. "You live here now."

Just then, she heard her parents' car drive in. "Don't make a sound," she warned, putting him back in the cupboard. "My parents would never let me keep you. In fact, the only way they'd let you stay is if they thought I *didn't* want you. Then they'd probably . . ."

Leeva sat back on her heels. Hmm. Harry had wondered if she might be a good actress. Perhaps tonight was the night to find out.

She prepared her parents' dinners, brought them into the living room, and sat silently until they'd finished.

Then she stood up and announced, "I have something to tell you."

Mr. Thornblossom snapped some batteries into his calculator.

Mrs. Thornblossom turned up the volume on her television.

Leeva drew herself up taller. "I'm *so glad* I don't have a pet!" she cried, adding a dramatic sweep of relief over her brow. "I sure would hate having a pet!"

Both her parents looked up at that. Tiny hot gleams burst in their eyes, like pinpoints of fire.

Her father put down his calculator. "So, you would hate having a little puppy or a kitten around, eh?"

"Well, I guess *those* would be all right," Leeva said. "It's a badger I was thinking about. I would really hate having a badger for a pet. Thank goodness I don't!"

"We're getting a badger," her mother said, with such a firm stomp of her heel that a cloud of crystal dust blew up.

"It can't cost anything," Mr. Thornblossom warned.

"Go get it yourself, Leeva," Mrs. Thornblossom said. "That's an order. Now stop talking and go away."

And Leeva did.

Back in the kitchen, she opened the sink cupboard.

Bob tumbled out, looking hungry. She opened the fridge wide and made an encouraging gesture. "Help yourself."

Bob climbed in. When he came upon a half-eaten Cheezaroni block, a pink tongue darted out and took a lick. His stubby tail thumped. He started gnawing.

Leeva settled down to watch from her thinking spot.

Bob, she mused. Had she been the person doing the naming, she'd have picked a hero from one of the books she'd read. But given the humiliation of the way she herself had been named, she was in no position to criticize.

"Do you mind being called Bob?" she asked the badger.

He looked up from the Cheezaroni block as if to say he didn't much care one way or the other about his name, but he certainly did care about eating this meal in peace, thank you very much.

Leeva, who had been so hungry before Harry's lunches and his aunt's cookies, empathized. She had walked Bob's path.

She leaned back between the cupboards and contemplated the turn her life had just taken. She had gone out this afternoon looking for some sesame seeds. She'd returned with those seeds. But she'd also returned with a badger.

Now, Reader, badgers never figure in to anyone's plans. "Oh, dear, I need some help, better go find a badger!" said exactly no one in the history of the world, ever. Because badgers are pretty appalling creatures: bad-tempered, malodorous, and related to skunks and weasels—unsavory family ties at best. No, a badger hadn't been part of her plan.

It all went to show that Harry had been right when he'd said that you couldn't predict what might happen when you set out for a new place.

Like coming home with a badger you were now responsible for.

The weight of this struck her. She'd had responsibilities before—pretty much from the time she could stand up, in fact. But being responsible for something alive—something that *relied* on her—felt different from being responsible for all the duties listed in her manual.

It felt like making a promise.

BOB EATS A GASKET

Leeva woke in an anxious cloud—an unfortunate side effect of responsibility. She hurried downstairs, flung open Bob's cupboard, and found that although he'd enlarged the hole in the floor, he was still there, phew, safe and sound.

His whiskers drooped, though, and his eyes were red and swollen, as if he might have been crying.

Leeva dropped to her knees. "Oh, Bob, I'm sorry. I left you all alone in a new place at night. I wouldn't like that if it happened to me. From now on, I'll bring you up to my room."

Leeva began her parents' breakfasts. While their coffee brewed, she sliced a grapefruit in half. She picked up the grapefruit spoon cautiously—the spoon's bowl was viciously serrated like sharks' teeth—and gouged out the grapefruit's sections, then arranged them on her mother's crystal plate. She folded a napkin just so and secured it with one of the glittery napkin rings her mother was favoring this month. Next, she sawed a Cheezaroni block in two and thunked one half on the tray for her father.

"Eat whatever you like," she urged Bob, propping open the refrigerator door. "I'll be right back."

She carried the breakfast tray out to the living room and served her parents.

"What's that?" her father asked. "On the floor, behind you."

Leeva looked down. There was Bob. Her heart thumped. But then her mother said, "That must be that badger we told her to get, Dolt. The one she said she'd hate to have."

Leeva recovered. "I hate it all right! It's the worst!"

"Good," her parents said at once, then turned to their programs.

Leeva sat on her stool with Bob on her lap, petting him secretly, trying to let him know she hadn't meant what she'd said. When her parents finished their meals, she brought their dishes to the kitchen, plunked Bob in the refrigerator again, and began cleaning up. When she'd dried the last cup, she turned to the refrigerator.

Bob was still in there, chomping noisily on a long black string. His eyes were closed in a manner that suggested bliss.

Leeva took a closer look. "That's the gasket, Bob," she groaned. "The rubber seal around the door that keeps the cold air in."

Bob swallowed the last bit. He did not look remorseful.

Leeva sighed. She picked up the remaining half block of Cheezaroni, scooped out the gummiest part, and pressed globs of it all around the edge of the door where the gasket had been. "Good as new," she declared.

She looked over at Bob. "But are you?"

Bob burped and curled up for a nap. This did not answer Leeva's concern one way or the other.

But she knew what would.

WHAT HARRY KNOWS

"Do you have any books on badgers?" Leeva asked when Harry appeared on the back stoop at noon.

Harry held up a just-a-second finger and went back in. He popped out with a stack of books almost immediately.

"How did you . . . ?" Leeva asked.

Harry smiled mischievously. "These were in the book return this morning, so apparently our patron no longer needs them. But now *you* do! What a coincidence."

Leeva drew the books close. She looked pointedly at Harry. "You know about Bob?"

Harry rolled his eyes skyward, the picture of innocence. He was a pretty good actor. But Leeva wasn't fooled. She frowned.

Harry laughed. "What I know is that if a certain small badger needed someone to take care of him, you'd be a good choice." He shook his head. "All that suffering, just because someone has to have a statue of herself!"

Leeva gulped at the reminder of what a Thornblossom had caused. It suddenly felt wrong that Harry didn't know who she was.

While Harry was gone fetching his lunch, Leeva deliberated. Should she tell him? If she did, would it change how he felt about her?

She *would* tell him, she decided finally. And she'd do it before Mrs. Flowers opened the window, so at least she wouldn't have to hear the name Thornblossom.

As soon as Harry came back out, she began. "Harry, does it matter to you what a person's relatives do?"

"Of course." Harry put the tray down and aimed his voice up toward the third floor. "It matters a lot! That's why I'm *so glad* I can help my aunt out!"

Leeva tried again. "But what if, say, the person's mother—"

Mrs. Flowers threw open the window and stuck out her head. "Remember, it's just for the summer, Harry. I'm sorry you have to do it at all, but I'll figure something out by the time you go off to London." An oven timer went off then and she disappeared.

Harry handed Leeva a grilled cheese sandwich on rye bread and a mug of creamy tomato soup. It smelled delicious again, but Leeva's stomach hurt from worry. "You haven't told her yet, have you?" she whispered.

Harry shook his head. "Not until the elevator's here."

"Do you really have to use your school money for it?"

Harry took a sip of soup. "I do. Those Thornblossoms."

"I'm really sorry."

"Now, why would you be sorry? You're not to blame."

Leeva swirled the soup in her mug. She wasn't to blame. Harry had said it as if he knew it was true. She really wanted to believe him.

Harry pulled a slip of paper from his pocket and passed it over. *One dried orange peel*, it said, with a new address. "And the map," he said, handing it to her. "Might as well keep it."

Just then, Mrs. Flowers reappeared and lowered her bucket. Nestled inside, cozy in their napkin, were three still-warm, golden cookies speckled all over with sesame seeds. "Aren't they pretty?" she sang. "*Champurradas*. They're Guatemalan."

"*Champurradas*. Thank you," Leeva said, though

the cookies made her feel even worse. She put them on top of her books, wondering: Would Mrs. Flowers have given them to her if she'd known her last name was Thornblossom? Would she be righteously indignated *at her* for the things her parents had done?

That thought did it. Harry and Pauline Flowers must never find out who she was.

A CURIOUS COINCIDENCE

As Leeva slid the badger books under her bed, it struck her that of course it was Osmund who'd taken them out, and for the same reason she had. He'd probably hidden them from his parents, too. She and Osmund had walked the same path.

Downstairs, she found Bob awake and scratching at the cupboard floor again. "I can't leave you alone, can I? Well then, you'll have to come with me today. Wait here. I'll make you a leash." Leeva left for the basement to get some twine. She knew she'd find it there because it was her job to bundle up the old *Nutsmore Weekly*s and store them. Her father only allowed the subscription because there were so many things he could use the old issues for, things that otherwise might have to be purchased.

If he had his way, everything in the house would be made of newspaper. Leeva's mother had put her foot down about using it for toilet paper, but she allowed his many other uses.

In winter, of course, he burned the issues for heat. In summer, he made Leeva fold them into fans and window shades. Except for his recliner, all the furniture on his side of the living room was made of newspapers, cleverly folded and taped by Leeva.

Leeva's things, too—her coverlet, her slippers, her stool—all newspaper. She'd used only the "Improve Your Vocabulary" pages for the stool's seat, and it brought her a secret joy to perch upon precious words, but the rest of the things were a disappointment—scratchy and frail.

At the basement door, Leeva paused to strap on her miner's headlamp. There were lights in the basement, but her father insisted she use the headlamp, to save on the cost of electricity. Then she made her way down the staircase.

As she cut three lengths of twine and braided them together, a curious coincidence struck her: on the top floor of her house was a room filled with *greenish* paper, and here on the bottom floor, one filled with *grayish* paper. How about that, hmm?

Leeva looped one end for a handle and brought the leash upstairs. Her gaze swept the kitchen and settled on the perfect collar: the glittery napkin ring was elastic.

Bob eyed the collar and leash suspiciously.

"Don't worry, I'll bring the backpack in case you get tired. Think of it as an adventure," she encouraged him, slipping the collar around his neck and tying on the leash. "We don't know what's going to happen."

The badger's eyes, already squinty, squinted further.

"Besides, we'll visit Osmund first. He's probably worrying about you." She put the map and the cookies into their own pockets in the backpack and slipped it over her shoulders. Once again, wearing it seemed to say *You can do it!*, which was nice to hear as she stood on the front step, confronting the first challenge: How to get to the sidewalk?

Unlike the spot in the backyard, her parents might

notice a disturbance in the hedge out front. And she couldn't just walk out the driveway, to be filmed by all their hidden cameras. No, her only real option was to use her regular exit.

She carried Bob to the hedge in the back, and after peering through it to be sure Harry wasn't at the window, she broke through, set Bob down, and headed for the street.

A LAND WHERE
NOTHING HAPPENS

Bob was not a speedy walker. His legs were short and he stopped to investigate many objects on the ground. Worms, which apparently were delicious; cigarette butts, which apparently were not. A smashed wren's egg, whose dried yolk made Leeva ponder the fragility of life; torn lottery tickets, which spoke of both optimism and desperation; a red clown nose, which defied interpretation. And on and on.

Leeva had walked this same route yesterday and completely missed these intriguing items, being so much taller. A great deal in life, apparently, depended on one's point of view.

When Osmund opened the door, he fell to his knees,

his paper suit crinkling joyfully. "Bob!" he cried, "Bob, oh, Bob!"

Leeva was touched by how tender their reunion was. "I went to the library for some books about badgers," she said after a bit. "I took out the ones you returned."

Osmund stood up. He nodded slightly.

"Just now," Leeva ventured, "when you found out that we took out the same books, did you *feel* something?"

Osmund took a step back. "Maybe."

"Like something invisible *stretching* between you and me?"

Osmund frowned. He hugged Bob even tighter to his chest. "Maybe," he repeated warily. "But I think my suit will protect me from it."

"I am not a hazardous material!"

Osmund eyed her doubtfully.

Insulted, Leeva took Bob's leash. "We're leaving. Mrs. Flowers needs a dried orange peel tomorrow. Goodbye."

"Wait. Stop. I . . . I'll go with you." Osmund raised a finger. "Because badgers are so dangerous."

"No!" Leeva did not want to spend one extra minute with someone who thought she was a hazardous material—who would? But then she thought of something that could make it worthwhile. "Well, all right. You can tell me about school on the way."

Osmund groaned, but he agreed. "Come in. I'll get ready." And he disappeared down a hallway.

Leeva heard a great deal of rustling and zipping and snapping. She wandered over to the table. Once more, a bunch of figurines were set up on a board. All were animals except one—an action figure caped in a surgical mask. Lettered across the board was the word *SAFETY-LAND*. Around the border ran a path of squares, and in the center were two small white cubes and a stack of cards labeled *DANGER*.

Leeva picked up a cube. Each side had a different number of dots on it, one through six. She plucked a card and turned it over, but before she could read it, she heard steps in the hall. She dropped the card and turned away from the table.

Osmund reappeared, wearing another hazmat suit—this one blue. He snugged the wrist bands. "Level C, graded for outdoor hazards," he assured Leeva, as though she'd been worried. He bent to lace up a pair of work boots. "Steel toes."

"Why? The place we're going is just on the other side of the park."

Well, Reader, that set him off. "Why? WHY?" he cried, throwing his arms around. "Rocks, poisonous snakes, falling trees! Asteroids, trains . . ."

"No, I was just out there, I didn't see any of those—"

"Do you know how much an elephant weighs? My feet could get run over by a truck full of elephants, and in these, I wouldn't feel a thing. Don't *you* . . ." He looked down at Leeva's feet and gaped in horror.

Leeva looked down, too, to see what was wrong.

Nothing was wrong. There were her sandals—a fairly new pair. She was proud of these shoes, which she fashioned by molding tinfoil Cheezaroni trays around her feet, then strapping them on with masking tape. In winter, she molded a second Cheezaroni tray over the top of each foot to keep the heat in. The shoes were never comfortable, and the tape left itchy bands around her ankles, but the silvery flash they made when they caught the light was lovely. Leeva lifted a foot to show him.

Osmund shook his head. "I'll get you a pair of my boots."

Leeva recalled the way the breeze had felt on her toes on the way over here, and how the soft grass had brushed her ankles. "No thank you."

Osmund shrugged. He put on a face shield and

earmuffs.

"How are you going to hear me, or tell me about school with those on?"

He tapped the face shield. "Two-way communication, built-in." Then he tugged on a pair of gloves.

"But how are you going to smell things and touch things?"

"Let's go," he muttered grimly, taking the leash from Leeva. He unlocked three locks, ushered her outside, then snapped the locks closed again.

Once they began walking, Leeva reminded him of his promise.

"Why haven't you ever been to school?" he asked. "You look old enough."

"I'm old enough. My parents don't want me to go."

"Why not?"

"Because they teach Human Inanities." Leeva thought back so she would get it right. "Things like art, literature, poetry, music. Things you don't need to get famous or make money."

Osmund stopped. He slumped so deeply his suit seemed to deflate. "Oh. I thought those were the Humanities. Things humans do for other humans, to make life better."

"No, sorry. Inanities means stupid things."

Osmund collapsed deeper. "I really like those things. They're the best thing about school. And they're really safe. It's rare to get hurt listening to music or watching a play."

"Sorry," Leeva said again. "I like the Human Inanities, too. Or at least books. I don't know the other things. But my mother says kids don't get money or fame from going to school. Is that right?"

Osmund picked up Bob and began to stroke him. "Well," he said after a thoughtful pause, "well, that might be true, but . . . it's harder to get famous or rich *without* going to school."

Leeva filed away this interesting answer for possible use in her argument for going to school. But right now, she wanted to know something else. The most important thing. "Are there lots of people in school?"

Osmund started walking again. "They're everywhere. Grown-ups and kids. In the classrooms, in the halls and the offices, in the cafeteria and the gymnasium, and outside on the playground. Everywhere."

"That sounds wonderful!"

Osmund shook his head morosely. "Not wonderful. You have to be on your guard every minute. With other risks, you know the odds. But people? They're unpredictable."

Leeva walked beside him for a moment, thinking. People *were* unpredictable, he was right about that. She'd seen it herself during her week in the library, and it was one of the things she liked best.

Once, for instance, an old man had come in, pulled a book off the shelf, and read a poem to himself. Tears had streamed down his face, but he'd been smiling. When he finished, he'd unclipped his bow tie and placed it on top of the book as he'd put it back on the shelf. Unpredictable, all right.

And even Osmund, right now. He'd called badgers

dangerous, yet here he was cuddling Bob. Who would have guessed? And that board with all the animals on it . . .

"What's SafetyLand?" she asked.

Osmund lifted his chin. "A board game I invented."

"How do you play?"

For the first time, Osmund seemed excited. "You pick an animal and guide it around the board by rolling the dice."

"Are dice the cubes with the dots?"

"Right. You move however many dots you see, then—"

"So, mostly seven spaces."

"What?"

"If you toss two cubes and each cube has one through six dots, the most common combination is a seven."

Osmund was quiet for a moment. "Huh . . . you're right," he said. "So when you go to that square, you turn over a card and find out what the danger is. Tar pits, plague, explosions, all the big ones."

"Wow, exciting. All those disasters happening."

"It is exciting. But the disasters don't happen. You avoid them. Like, if I picked up the earthquake card and I was the duck, I'd say, 'Fly.' But if I was the turtle, I'd say,

'Tuck into my shell.'"

"Huh. So nothing happens?"

Osmund nodded. "If you play it right."

"What's the doll for?"

"That's Osmundio. He's a superhero. His name means 'divine protector.' If you can't think of a way out of a disaster, you say, 'Protect us, Osmundio!' three times and he makes everything safe."

"I don't get it. Who wants to play a game where nothing happens?"

Osmund slumped. "Nobody."

"You asked people?"

"At first. But I don't anymore." He turned away. "Never mind."

Leeva felt bad. "No, explain it to me again."

Osmund shook his head. He pointed to a large house. "That's the address," he said. "We're here."

THE GIRL WITH THE BRAID IN THE BACK

The house was tired-looking, but it was wrapped in a welcoming porch. Leeva took a step forward.

Osmund took a step back. "Do you know the people who live there?"

"Not yet. But Harry does, and he sent me here."

"Harry . . . Well, then, it must be okay." Osmund followed Leeva to the steps but refused to go farther.

Leeva climbed onto the porch and knocked. The door flew open and a bunch of little kids tumbled out in a shouty tangle. One of them popped her head up. "That's the worst dog I ever saw," she yelled, pointing at Bob.

Well, that brought Osmund stomping up the steps. "He's a badger, and he's a great one!"

Just then, the smallest kid sailed over the railing and landed in a rosebush with a yelp.

The yelp brought a girl about Leeva's size to the door. "Not again," she sighed, then placed a book on the railing and went after the little boy.

As she passed, Leeva's jaw fell open. The girl had a braid. A single perfect braid, every glossy black hair in place. *In the back!*

When the girl carried the little boy onto the porch, Osmund elbowed Leeva. "Get that orange peel and let's go."

Leeva couldn't. Not yet. She lifted her own two ragged braids toward the girl. "How do you do yours so neat behind yourself?"

The girl dropped her squirming brother. "*I* don't. My father does it before he goes to work. Sometimes my mother."

Leeva nodded, too surprised to speak. She had first seen braids on a child star years before in *Celebrities This Week* magazine. In the photo, the child star's parents were gazing down at her adoringly, each with a hand on her shoulder, beside a braid. Leeva had studied the picture until she had figured out how to arrange her own hair like that. Perhaps then, she'd hoped, her parents would gaze at her adoringly, or at least rest their hands on her shoulders.

Neither of those things happened. But the way the new braids rested on her shoulders had felt reassuring, the way she imagined parents' hands would, and so she'd kept them.

Osmund nudged her from behind. "Come *on*."

Leeva ignored the nudge. "Someone else could braid your hair," she murmured. "Someone's *parents* could do it."

"Your parents *don't*?" the girl asked.

"Let's go," Osmund hissed to Leeva.

"Okay." Leeva pushed her braids to her back and began. "Hello, my name is Leeva and I'm on a mission of utmost importance."

The girl smiled and saluted. "I'm Fern. What's the mission?"

"Fern! Like in *Charlotte's Web*. I loved that book!"

"Me, too!" Fern cried. "Except the end . . . oh . . ." She wiped away imaginary tears.

"Me, too!" Leeva agreed. "The mission is: Harry Flowers sent me to ask for a dried orange peel, please. It's for his aunt. For her cookies."

Fern curtsied. "Of course," she said. She picked up her book. "Come in. But just *you*!"

"I don't want to come in anyway," Osmund muttered. He tied Bob to the railing and Leeva followed Fern inside.

TEARS UNDER THE BUSH

Fern brought Leeva into a kitchen filled with a strange, sharp odor. An extremely old couple sat sprawled over a kitchen table, sleeping—or maybe they'd passed out from the odor, that's how strong it was.

"My great-grandparents," Fern said. She placed her book on the table and gently turned the woman's head to face Leeva. "This girl would like a dried orange peel."

The extremely old woman nodded as if she approved.

"It's of the utmost importance," Leeva added.

The extremely old man opened his eyes and raised a finger. "Utmost importance, that's the ticket."

Fern climbed onto the counter and took a jar from a shelf. "Orange peels." After pulling out a long, brown, spiraling peel, she hopped down, wrapped it in waxed paper, and handed it to Leeva.

The old people were snoring again. Fern patted each of their heads, which made Leeva's throat hurt for some reason. Then Fern picked up a long-handled spoon and brought it to the stove, where a big pot of green slop was blopping away.

"Careful, it stains," she said when Leeva peered over her shoulder. "Dandelion stew. My great-grandparents like it, but phew . . ." She pinched her nose in a way that Leeva found hilariously tragic.

It occurred to Leeva that Harry would probably admire this girl's acting ability. Maybe he'd invite her to try out for that part in that play.

The thought struck a surprising cold sting in her heart.

At a shriek from the living room, Fern turned off the stove and sighed. "My brothers and sisters. I can't leave any of them for a minute." She looked longingly at her book, then started down the hall.

Leeva knew how difficult it was to leave a book you were reading. She had walked that path. She wished she could offer a solution. But she could already see that Fern's problem was a difficult one: how to watch over people of vastly different age—

"I have an idea!" Leeva hurried to Fern at the living room doorway. Inside, little kids were launching themselves from couches to chairs to tables and back again. Before she could speak, one of the little girls pulled a set of drapes onto herself and sailed into a bookcase.

Fern rescued her sister with extravagant sighing and eye-rolling, and Leeva thought again that Harry should know about this girl. Once more, she felt an odd freeze in her chest.

Fern looked up from untangling the drapes. "You said you had an idea?"

"Oh, right. I know a television show, *Vim and Vigor at Any Age.* I think both your great-grandparents and your brothers and sisters would enjoy it. Maybe you could get some time to read."

Fern's eyes widened. "Let's try it." She went back into the kitchen and woke her great-grandparents gently, then steered them into the living room. Leeva stationed herself between them, ready to catch them if they went over, while Fern found the program and lined up her brothers and sisters.

Trainers Jilly and Jim were leading a round of lunges.

"You can do it," they cheered. "You are vimful and vigorous!"

The two old people perked up when they heard this. They dove in and the little kids followed. Rugs skittered and lamps wobbled.

"Are you sure this is a good idea?" Fern asked.

"It's *Vim and Vigor at Any Age*," Leeva assured her. She went back to get Fern's book. It was *Mrs. Frisby and the Rats of NIMH*. "I loved this," she said as she held it out. "But the plow!"

"The plow!" Fern said at exactly the same time, with a look that reflected the same horror Leeva had felt. As she took the book, Fern dropped her head and looked up at Leeva through her bangs. "You could come back, maybe. I can't leave, but if this works, I could visit with you here while the show is on." She looked over at her family—nine people jumping happily in unison—and then she raised a hand and crossed her first two fingers. "You could come back anytime."

Leeva could tell from Fern's expression that the intriguing gesture was a wish for good luck. She raised her own hand and crossed her fingers in the same secret symbol.

The two of them tiptoed out to the porch, Leeva thinking happily that yes, maybe she *would* come back. "Well, thanks for the orange peel," she said. "Harry will be happy."

The girl pressed her book to her heart. "Harry's great. He reads my brothers and sisters stories and acts out all the parts so they'll behave while I pick out my books."

Leeva tried to imagine the jumble of kids in the library. "You bring them all?"

"Yes, but it's not their fault."

"What isn't?" Leeva asked.

Fern nodded inside. "That I have to watch them all, that I can't go anywhere without them. Everybody old enough in my family is working. My parents, my grandparents, even my older sister. I miss her so much. I miss them all so much." She frowned. "Those *Thornblossoms!*"

Leeva reared back as if she had been kicked in the chest. "The Thornblossoms?" she asked when she'd caught a breath.

"They charged us a Tax-Challenging Tax just because my parents asked why the taxes were so high!"

Well, Reader, Leeva couldn't take it. She grabbed Bob, bolted off the steps, and ran down the sidewalk as fast as she could. When she was sure she couldn't be seen anymore, she dove under a bush.

There, in the dirt and the dark and the prickers, she wept—the name Thornblossom, *her* name, was poison in this town!—until hot mud puddled on her cheeks. As she mopped at it with the collar of her blouse, her fingers tangled in the twine around her neck.

Her sobbing ebbed. Hope flowed in.

Leeva pulled out the library card. "Do you know what this is, Bob?"

Bob sniffed it intently but did not seem to come to a conclusion.

"It's a card of trust. That says something, doesn't it? You can trust me, too. Bob, I am going to make Thornblossom a name we can both be proud of."

Leeva crawled out from under the briars. The sun felt bright and comforting on her shoulders.

But there stood Osmund, looking down at her.

THE GIFT

"I was worried about you," Osmund said. "You were in that house so long. And then you ran away."

"You were waiting for me? Then you followed me?"

"I was worried. Bad things happen."

Osmund didn't say anything more as he followed Leeva out onto the sidewalk, carrying Bob. When they reached his house, though, he said, "You have dirt and leaves in your hair. Wait here." And then he went into his parents' office.

When he came back out, he handed Leeva a comb wrapped in cellophane.

"For me?"

Osmund shrugged as if the gift was not a big deal.

But it was a big deal. Red plastic, stamped in gold

with the slogan *Frisk Insurance, Let Us Untangle Your Insurance Needs!*, the comb was beautiful. But more importantly, it was the first thing Leeva had ever been given that was to be all hers forever. Even her clothes were only a loan—her father kept a ledger and she was expected to pay for them when she got a job.

Leeva stood on the sidewalk for a moment, cradling the gift. And then she unwrapped it and began to comb out her tear-salted, muddied, finger-plaited-by-herself braids.

"That's better," Osmund said, and then he left.

Leeva placed the comb carefully into its own pouch in the backpack and walked to the library with her head held high.

Harry wasn't out on the stoop, so she sat down to wait. Mrs. Flowers threw open the window and leaned out. "Would you do me a favor, Leeva?"

Leeva jumped up. Of course she would!

"Harry had to go early and he didn't have time to water my herbs. Would you do it? The spigot is around the corner, across from the book drop."

Leeva found the spigot and filled the watering can beneath it. When she'd soaked the last pot, Mrs. Flowers waved down at her. "Thank you, my dear."

Well, Leeva nearly dropped the watering can. Had Mrs. Flowers just called her *my dear*, the way Grandmother Cleverton addressed her twin granddaughters, whom she loved?

Leeva pulled out the orange peel and placed it on the table. "I'll leave it here, okay?"

"Wonderful, thank you. Orange biscotti tomorrow—I hope you like them, my dear."

My dear! Again!

Leeva walked back to her house pondering life. One minute you're weeping in the mud under a pricker bush, the next you're someone's dear, with a brand-new comb. Life.

THE ELEVATOR ARRIVES

Around midnight, Leeva awoke to a frantic scrab-
bling under her bed. She turned on her lamp and
hung over the side to look.

"Bob! What are you doing?"

Bob looked up with an expression that clearly said,
What did you expect, I'm a badger.

Leeva got out of bed to examine the damage. In one
spot, Bob had scraped clear through the floorboards to
the kitchen below. Another week and her bed would
fall right through onto the stove. In the unlikely event
one of her parents happened to be cooking a midnight
snack, she would be fricasseed, a fate even Osmund's
parents had failed to warn her about.

Leeva pulled Bob out and consulted *Badger Behavior*.

Badgers were night creatures, it confirmed. They were born to dig, and dig they must.

Leeva tiptoed downstairs and out to the backyard, where a few holes wouldn't be noticed, and sat beside him as he tore into the dirt. Watching him gobble earthworms by the light of a half moon, she sighed deeply.

Compared to the many pets she read about in her library books, Bob was a dud. He slept most of the day, and when he wasn't sleeping, he mainly waddled around and dug holes. His disposition was uniformly crabby. He showed almost no interest in Leeva at all, and when he did, he always seemed kind of judgmental. Whatever Leeva did, he seemed to raise a skeptical eyebrow, as if *he* wouldn't be caught dead doing such a ridiculous thing.

In spite of all this, she found herself growing more and more fond of him. The crabbier, the more judgmental he acted, the more she wanted to defend him, to cheer him on in his judgmental crabbiness. It was all very confusing.

Well, what mattered was that she had a badger who could no longer be left alone in the house at all. Leeva curled up on the ground and fell into a light, worried sleep while he dug.

The next day, Leeva brought Bob with her to the library at noon. She tied him to a board on the back stoop and held her breath when Harry came outside with his lunch tray.

Harry looked at Bob. Then he looked at Leeva. Then he pressed his mouth into a tight line and said nothing as he set down the tray.

Leeva made a mental note: Sometimes, *nothing* is exactly what you want to hear.

Harry motioned to the tray. On it were three muffins, three hard-boiled eggs, and three tall glasses of orange juice. "It's brunch, actually," Harry explained. "We didn't have time for breakfast, what with all of the commotion this morning."

Before Leeva could ask *What commotion?* and *Why do you have three of everything?*, the library's back door opened again.

And out walked Mrs. Flowers!

"What? How?" Leeva managed.

Pauline Flowers's face lit up. "I've had the best surprise! An elevator! Harry had it installed last night. I'll be working as a librarian again, beginning today!" She beamed at her nephew.

Harry looked happy, too. But Leeva wondered: Were there two Harrys—one proud he'd given his aunt her dream, and one grieving because he'd given up his own?

Harry was apparently thinking about that, too. "Since I won't be needed here, I've signed up for acting classes at the Community Theater. Now, Leeva, come inside for just a minute, take a ride in the new elevator. It's really fun."

"Yes, go try it," Mrs. Flowers urged. "There's a famous poem: It goes, 'Oh! I have slipped the surly bonds of Earth,' and you'll know just what it means when you press Up."

Leeva walked over to the door. There, though, she stopped. Her mother was extraordinarily skilled at punishing people. And if someone ignored one of her punishments, she escalated. "No, I'd better not go in," she sighed at last.

"Well, at least have a look?" Harry opened the door wide.

Keeping her feet firmly outside, Leeva leaned in. There, in the center of the library, stood a huge, sleek silver tube.

Harry went in and pushed a button on the tube. A door slid open silently. He stepped in. The door slid shut with a silky click. Then Leeva heard a quiet, but thrilling *WHOOSH!*

Next thing she knew, Harry was grinning down at her over the railing in the nonfiction section. Her heart strained against her ribs. She wanted so much to take a ride. She felt a hand on her back.

"Someday," Mrs. Flowers said kindly.

"Maybe," Leeva said, although she didn't believe it.

Harry came back and passed out the food. Leeva sat next to him as usual, but she edged a little closer to Mrs. Flowers's chair. It was nice to not have to shout, and to see her up close. Today the librarian's reading glasses were shaped like scallop shells. Her earrings were silver books, with tiny strings of red beads for bookmarks. And she smelled wonderfully of vanilla and baked sugar, which Leeva would not have been able to enjoy from far below.

As she finished her muffin, Leeva realized something. "I guess I won't see you much, Harry." She took a swallow of orange juice, because her throat had suddenly gone dry.

"Oh, no, don't worry. I'll be upstairs in the mornings. I'm trying my hand at writing a play. And my classes are in the afternoon. I wouldn't miss lunch with you." He got up, brushed the muffin crumbs off his pants, and brought the dishes inside.

Leeva turned to Mrs. Flowers. "And you?" Her voice was a little quivery.

"I'll be right here at noon each day."

"And will you still . . ." Leeva glanced at the cookies.

"Of course! It's a life goal! I'll just get up a little earlier to bake them." But then her expression changed. "You know, I'm happy about the elevator. But I'm still quite angry."

"At what?" Leeva asked.

"We should have had that elevator years ago. And I'm not at all happy that Harry used his school money. I will not allow him to give up that opportunity. Somehow we'll have to find another ten thousand dollars by the time school starts."

It suddenly felt wrong that Mrs. Flowers didn't know who she was. It felt like a lie. *My last name is Thornblossom, and my parents are the reason you didn't get that elevator before,* she ought to say. *If they'd let you buy it, Harry would still have his school money.*

Leeva put down her glass. She *would* say it, no matter the cost. But as she opened her mouth, Mrs. Flowers spoke again.

"The people who hold the keys, who lie and cheat to get those keys, who clutch those keys in a death grip—why won't they use them to unlock the doors? Do you ever wonder about that, Leeva?"

Leeva pictured the locked room beside her bedroom, stuffed with money. She thought about all the rules in her Employee Manual. "I do wonder that," she said.

"I thought you might." Mrs. Flowers shook her head so hard her earrings jangled. "Well, today we're celebrating. I'm working as a librarian once more."

Leeva got up to peer at the elevator again. "Where did the books go? The ones that used to be where the elevator is now?"

"Boxed up. Downstairs, in fiction, it was the cookbooks. They didn't really belong in fiction anyway. I can fetch them when anyone asks."

Harry returned just then. He handed Leeva a slip of paper with the day's address on it.

"And upstairs, in the informational texts," Mrs.

Flowers said, "it was only some town reports. Nobody took those out."

"Just a bunch of confusing numbers," Harry agreed, chuckling. "Who would ever read those?"

HAPPY DAYS

The next week was the happiest of Leeva's life.

She found that if she fitted Bob's paws with tiny Cheezaroni-tray booties, he would give up digging and sleep most of the night. In the mornings, she raced through her chores, exercised with *Vim and Vigor at Any Age*, then took him out in her backyard, where she read beside him as he dug.

The word of that week was *Luminescence—the emission of light by an object that has not been heated.* It was a lovely word and she looked forward to using it.

Harry and Pauline Flowers spent every lunch hour with her and shared their delicious meals. Then Mrs. Flowers brought out three fresh cookies and ten new books. She began mixing some nonfiction in with the stories, and Leeva's sharp mind polished itself on a wealth of fascinating information. She learned all the constellations and memorized the periodic table of elements and read up on all 195 countries. By the end of that week, she could recite the depths of all the lakes in the world, the heights of the mountains, the lengths of the rivers, the salinity of the seas.

At one o'clock each day, rain or shine, Osmund was waiting in front of the library. He always claimed he was there strictly in case Bob's badger nature became a problem—"You never heard of a *good*ger, did you?"—but Leeva knew this was an excuse. And she didn't mind him tagging along. No matter what happened, it was better with someone else there, even with Osmund, as long as she ignored his gloomy mutterings about the odds of this or that tragedy wrecking things.

Harry had been right: She met a wide variety of people when she went on her errands. Though they were wildly different, all of them were happy to contribute whatever Mrs. Flowers needed for her cookies. And at every encounter, Leeva collected another bit of evidence of what people were for, mostly in the form of a story about Harry.

Osmund was sure that Bob was homesick, so after

getting the day's ingredient, they always brought him to the park.

The first day they'd done it, Leeva had let Bob off the leash at the scraped bare patch—how much trouble could one little badger make?

But Osmund had yelled in horror. "Rusty nails, pesticides, wolverines, I don't know what else! Bring him back!"

"He'll be fine, I do it all the time at my place. And he loves to dig. Watch."

Sure enough, Bob went bonkers digging around where he used to live, and anyone could see he was happy. Osmund couldn't argue with that, so after the first day, he didn't—he only watched over Bob carefully and scowled at the bare spot until he went home.

Evenings back at Leeva's house were still pretty miserable. She had stopped doing the dishes and left them for Bob to lick clean, so that was an improvement. And now that she had so many people to talk with each day, she was no longer bothered when her parents ignored her. In fact, she wished they'd ignore her more. Because the more people she met, the more awful her parents seemed in comparison. Several times over that week, in fact, Leeva thought of running away. But deep down, she feared she wasn't brave enough to set off into the world on her own. Besides, where would she go?

Well, luckily, the days were long and the evenings in her house were short, and after dinner, Leeva was free to read her books upstairs with Bob, so all in all, the week was entirely wonderful.

Well . . . no. Not *entirely* wonderful, Reader. One thing was less than perfect: Each afternoon in the park, Leeva shared her cookies with Osmund.

Now, Leeva was happy to share. The cookies tasted even better when she shared them. Everything does. But the simple, undeniable fact was, she preferred three cookies to one and a half cookies. You understand.

And so one evening, when Leeva gave Harry the empty napkin, she hinted, "Um . . . you know, Osmund comes with me."

"Well, who *wouldn't* want to go with you?" Harry said. "Now, Aunt Pauline and I want to know: How did you like *Hamlet*?"

"I liked it very much." Leeva cleared her throat, which did not need clearing. "Maybe you could tell *your aunt* that Osmund goes with me," she suggested.

"I'll certainly mention it. She'll be as glad as I am. Now, Shakespeare—that guy had a lot to say. I think you'll like *A Midsummer Night's Dream* as well."

"Maybe." Frustrated, Leeva climbed up onto the table and looked right into his eyes. "Every day, I share my cookies with Osmund." She arched her eyebrows and added a meaningful smile.

"That's so nice. Aunt Pauline will get you that play tomorrow." Then Harry stepped off the stoop.

Time after time, in hundreds of episodes, Leeva had observed the characters on *The Winds of Our Tides* get the things they wanted by hinting. By suggesting. By arching their eyebrows and smiling in the meaningful manner that Leeva practiced in the mirror. But now it struck her: Nothing that happened in her soap opera ever happened to her.

Well, she figured, maybe you have to come right out and say what you want sometimes.

"Excuse me, Harry," she said. And then she waited. Only when he turned around and really looked at her did she continue. "Could I please have some *more* cookies, now that I'm sharing them?"

Harry waved his hands, as if the request was nothing. "Sure, sure! She's always looking to give her baking away."

After that, each day, Mrs. Flowers handed Leeva a

round blue tin decorated with snowmen and sparkly little snow mice. Inside were a *dozen* cookies. Leeva and Osmund now had three apiece in the park, and Leeva ate the other six reading her books in bed each night, and so the rest of the week *was* entirely wonderful.

It couldn't last, of course.

CAUGHT!

Ever since she'd been forbidden to go into the library, Leeva had hidden her books in her bedroom. It felt wrong that she should have to do this, as if she was ashamed of them. But at the same time, the secrecy made them more enjoyable.

Another thing that made the books more enjoyable: Sprinkled around their scenes were some of the words she'd learned from years of reading the "Improve Your Vocabulary" column filler. Each time one showed up, she greeted it with a cry of recognition.

And that, Reader, was how she got caught.

Lying in bed with Bob curled by her side, deep into *The Golden Compass*, she came upon the word *crypt*. *Crypt* was a terrific word on its own—an underground chamber used to store bodies!—but it was also the very first word she'd learned from the column, and so it held a special place in her heart. Her delighted "Hi, you!" must have been a shade too loud, because next thing she knew, there came a splintering kick to her door.

Leeva had a *second* to decide: Hide Bob, or hide the books. Whichever her parents thought had caused that happy cry would be taken from her.

She made her decision just as the door crashed open.

There stood her parents, her father blinking sleepily, her mother crossing her arms over her nightgown and tapping her stilettos. "Was that *happiness* I heard?" she asked.

Leeva gulped. "Yes."

Clink-clink-clink. Her mother drew closer. "Are those *books* I see?"

Leeva shrank down under her newspaper coverlet. She nodded.

Clink-clink. "*Library* books?"

"Yes. But I obey you! I don't go inside, Mother. The librarian brings the books *outside*."

Her father, slumped against the doorway, opened one eye. "And the money?"

"There's no money," Leeva answered. "It's a *library*. They lend you *books*. And I stay outside. Behind the library."

Her father seemed to awaken at that. "Behind the library? So, you left the yard?" And then Dolton Thornblossom had one of his fleeting moments of clear thought. He perked his eyebrows. He snapped his fingers. "But the Employee Manual. No leaving the workplace."

Mrs. Thornblossom actually jumped. "That's it! What's the punishment?"

Mr. Thornblossom's face slumped back into its usual expression of befuddlement. When his wife jerked her head in the direction of the living room below, he left. Leeva heard his heavy footsteps take the stairs and clomp to his recliner. When he returned a moment later with the manual, he was red-faced and panting—Dolton Thornblossom was neither vimful nor vigorous.

He thumbed through the pages. "Cut her salary," he read.

Leeva's mother waved this aside. "She has no salary."

"Cancel her vacation."

"She has no vacations."

"Withhold benefits? No bonus?" Mr. Thornblossom tried. "Fire her?"

Leeva had had it. No other kids even had an Employee Manual, she was sure of that now. "Fire me?" she cried. "From what job?"

"The job of being parented by us," her mother replied. She reached over and snapped the manual shut. "Put it back," she told her husband. "I'll decide on a punishment myself."

Leeva's father lumbered out.

Mayor Thornblossom spun to Leeva. "Obviously you're not to leave the workplace ever again. I'll let you know what your punishment is tomorrow." Then she left.

Leeva sat on her bed, rigid and quaking. Her jaw clenched so hard she thought her teeth might crack. The thing in her chest was beating its fists against her ribs.

She was on fire with righteous indignation. Tomorrow's punishment was going to be horrible, but that wasn't what had lit the match.

Obviously you're not to leave the workplace ever again.

Her mother's decree was simply impossible to even consider.

Because Reader, you can't put an oak tree back into the acorn.

You can't put a rainstorm back into the cloud.

You can't put a milkshake back into the cow.

You get the point. Leeva had gone out into the world, and she wasn't going to stuff herself back into her old cramped life. She could not do it. And she wouldn't.

She pulled Bob out from under the bed. "Maybe I'm not brave enough. Maybe I don't know where to go," she whispered into his ear. "But I am going to act with boldness and laser-like speed. Ready or not, Bob Thornblossom, we're running away."

LEEVA RUNS AWAY

Leeva waited until she heard both of her parents snoring. Inch by inch, she eased herself out of bed without rustling her newspaper coverlet. She dressed silently and then silently pulled Osmund's backpack from her closet.

Her map and her precious comb were already inside, each in its own zippered pouch. Leeva stacked her library books and the empty cookie tin into the main compartment—they must be returned before she got too far away. She added pajamas, a change of clothes, her toothbrush and toothpaste, and the onion bag that held the leftover scrids from her mother's fancy soaps. She hooked on Bob's leash, settled him on top, and then shouldered the pack. Its firm weight reassured her—she had a purpose, all right. She could do this, all right.

Maybe.

Pressing against the wall, where the steps didn't creak, she crept downstairs barefoot. At the basement door, she strapped on her headlamp, then hurried down and cut several lengths of twine. Bob chewed through his leashes pretty quickly.

Back upstairs, her gaze swept the kitchen. She opened the refrigerator door, stared in dismay for a moment, and then closed it. She would never be hungry enough to put that stuff into her mouth again. She quickly molded two fresh Cheezaroni trays to her feet and taped them on, then slipped the roll of tape into the backpack.

Leeva had one final thing to do. She tiptoed into the living room and over to her father's recliner. From its pocket, she withdrew her Employee Manual and the pen. Across the cover, in big bold letters, she scrawled *I quit!*, then put back the manual and slid the pen into her pocket.

Leeva twisted around to check on Bob. The badger's eyes were huge. "Don't worry," she whispered, gently pushing his head back down and zipping him in. "I'll take care of you."

And then Leeva Thornblossom stepped out the back door.

Above her stretched the wide indigo heavens. There was the Big Dipper, there was Orion, just as the book of constellations had shown, but so much more magnificent. She wanted to drop to the cool ground and drink in every star, but no, that would have to wait.

Leeva ran to the hedge and broke through at her usual spot.

But now where?

She pulled out her map and spread it out on the book drop, training her headlamp over the streets she knew so well now. They all seemed to beckon.

She wanted to stay fairly close to the library—she would need Harry and his aunt, and those lunches, more than ever. In fact, if she could, she'd hide out *in* the library. She looked across at its dark windows with longing—all those pillows and commodious chairs, and all those books! But of course, even if she could get in, she wouldn't risk it. A crucial part of running away was not getting caught.

What she needed was a secret place to spend the nights, a place where no one would think to look for her. It didn't have to be large, it only needed to be comfortable enough to curl up in, and sturdy enough to shelter her from hazards like storms.

As if she'd called one up, Leeva heard thunder rumble in the distance. She looked up—the stars had disappeared behind a layer of scudding clouds.

A sharp wind snapped the map. It smelled of rain.

Her library books! She'd better get them into the book drop, where they'd be safe and dry on that quilt—

The words struck her: Safe and dry! On a quilt!

Leeva aimed her headlamp at the keypad, pressed the numbers she remembered Harry using, and jumped inside just as the first raindrops spattered her neck.

IN THE BOOK DROP

Leeva worked her pen into the hinge so she wouldn't get locked in, then pulled the door closed. Outside, thunder boomed and rain began to bucket down. Leeva wormed off her backpack and pulled Bob out. He was shivering with fright, so she held him close as she examined the space by the light of the headlamp.

The book drop wasn't commodious by any means, but it was larger than she'd expected. In fact, it was just about the size and shape of her thinking spot, and she was always comfortable there. She rearranged the returned books in one corner to make more room, then smoothed the quilt over her lap.

The quilt was a faded yellow-and-white checked pattern. It was softer than anything she had ever touched before. Leeva wondered—had Harry slept under this quilt as a little boy? Last week, he had told her that his aunt had taken him in when he was only two, after a tragic accident—hippopotamuses run amok—had squashed his parents. The quilt's blue satin border was worn completely away in one place—had Harry rubbed it for comfort as Leeva was doing now?

Just then, a car drove up. Leeva tucked Bob under one arm and covered her head with the other as one, two, three books dropped in.

The car drove off and Leeva picked up the new books. They were all detective stories, so she chose the one with the most exciting cover—you can tell a lot about a book by its cover—and began to read.

As the storm abated, she congratulated herself on her shelter strategy. Fresh air slipped in through the book chute, which was cleverly angled downward so not a drop of rain entered. It was a relief to know that her parents wouldn't come barging in, and comforting that Harry and his aunt were close by. In fact, other than the occasional head-thunk, the book drop was very pleasant. After the misery of earlier in the evening, she was actually feeling happy.

Bob, however, was not. He sniffed the book drop's

walls more and more frantically, as if desperate to get out.

Leeva put herself in his place—something one should do, her instinct told her, when one was responsible for another being. Nights were still Bob's days, his time to be active. "You must feel claustrophobic in here," she said.

As if to prove it, Bob started clawing. The pretty quilt would be sliced to ribbons if she left him to it. Leeva looped the leash securely around her wrist and opened the big door. It was still raining, but more gently

now. She lifted Bob out and nudged him under the book drop. "Go dig yourself a nest." She pulled the door closed. "Good night," she called through the crack.

Leeva changed into her pajamas—not easy in a space the size of a missing dishwasher—and then pulled the quilt around her, plumped her backpack for a pillow, and opened the detective story. When she reached The End, she clicked off her headlamp and fell asleep to the patter of rain on the metal roof.

A FRESH START

Leeva awoke remarkably refreshed to the Town Hall clock striking seven. She dressed quickly, putting extra tape around her sandals, and climbed out with her possessions in her backpack.

The day was sunny—a rinsed-clean start for her new life. She scooped up Bob, who was just curling up for a nap in the burrow he'd dug under the book drop. "Sorry, no, we have to leave," Leeva told him. "Harry collects the books soon."

She brought him across the drive to the faucet, and they both drank their fill. Then, using the trowel that lived in a pot of parsley, Leeva scooped back all the earth Bob had excavated and covered the area with pine needles from under the hedge.

"Now," she said, "we have five hours until we can come back here for lunch. Where should we spend them?"

Bob yawned unhelpfully. But suddenly something wonderful occurred to Leeva: She had quit! She no longer had to obey her parents at all! Which meant she could walk right into the Nutsmore Public Library, right through the front doors as soon as the library opened at nine, just like any other Nutsmorian!

"We only have *two* hours to fill," she told Bob, settling him into the backpack. She hurried to the public bathrooms in the park, and finding no one else there, she ran water over her bag of soap scrids and scrubbed up as best she could. She brushed her teeth and combed and braided her hair.

As she left, the Town Hall clock struck eight. This close, the peals seemed to ring in her bones. This was a pleasant sensation, but it reminded her of something *un*pleasant: Her parents were due at their offices about now. She stepped behind a clump of trees, her heart pounding.

But . . . would they even go to work today? Surely they had noticed she was missing by now. They would have searched the house and called the police—that was the first thing worried families did in her books. Soon Nutsmore would be plastered with reward posters, swarming with search parties.

This thought was surprisingly satisfying, but it was also a complication Leeva had not considered.

She consulted her map and plotted out a long, isolated route back to the library. As she walked, she kept her ears sharpened for sirens, and though she never heard any, she jumped behind a tree trunk or flattened herself into brush whenever any vehicle approached.

Leeva was at the library's front doors when Mrs. Flowers opened them at nine.

"You're coming inside—what a nice surprise!" the librarian said. "No more punishment?"

"No," Leeva answered, walking in. "That's all over." She took out her ten books and piled them on the return desk.

"Well, thank goodness. And that means you can choose your own books! What a pleasure that is. I'll leave you to it, just call if you have any questions."

Leeva had never before been anywhere she could take whatever she wanted—*whatever she wanted!* Where to start? She looked around. The elevator caught her eye.

She dashed over to it, stepped in, and pressed Up.

She wasn't sure about escaping any surly bonds, but Harry was right—it was definitely *fun*. Up and down, up and down she rode, until at last she stepped out on the nonfiction floor and began selecting books on wilderness survival—if she was going to live on her own in a book drop, she'd better get prepared. She brought the books downstairs, checked them out, then chose an armchair by a window so she could keep an eye out for search parties and bolt out the back door if one appeared. She read, Bob snoring in the backpack at her feet, until Harry walked out of the elevator with lunch.

"Inside! Good for you!" he cheered when he caught sight of Leeva. "Hang out the Closed sign, okay?"

Leeva did and then followed him and his aunt to the stoop. Lunch was delicious and Leeva ate all she could. Reader, running away in the middle of the night gives one an appetite.

Harry brought out a bowl of cherries, and as they ate them, they competed to see how far they could spit the pits. Mrs. Flowers won every round. She took a little bow, then turned to Leeva. "How are you doing with your question? Have you found out what people are for?"

Leeva considered. She'd learned a lot of things people were for over the last weeks. Suddenly, she saw that they were all really the same thing. "Sharing," she said. "Everything that happens is better when someone else shares it with you. Happiness, sadness, being scared, being excited. Even this!" She shot her last pit clear over the driveway. "Spitting!"

Mrs. Flowers's earrings jangled, she nodded so vigorously. "Well put. Oh, Leeva, I'm going to miss these lunchtimes when school starts. You'll have to promise to visit after school."

Leeva put down her glass of lemonade. She was about to explain her tragic situation, no school, when she realized: There was no one to stop her now. Of course, by winter she would have to find a better place to live than the book drop—somewhere warm, with room to do homework—but that was a problem for later. "I'll be going to school," she said, shivering with the thrill of it.

"Yes, it's going to be lonely here in a few weeks," Mrs. Flowers went on, "with *both* of you gone." She aimed a determined look at Harry. "Harry off in London, somehow. Well, I'd better go in and get your cookies."

When she heard the elevator door had closed behind the librarian, Leeva leaned in toward Harry. "She still thinks you can go. Can you?"

Harry shook his head sadly. "I don't see how," he

said with a smile that only made Leeva feel sadder. "But I'll get a job in town, save my money. Maybe in a few years . . ." He stopped talking when his aunt came back out.

Besides the cookie tin, she handed Leeva a tall metal canister.

"What's this?"

"Milk. Very cold, and the thermos will keep it that way. I'm sorry I didn't think of it before. You're going to have cookies, you need cold milk."

"Actually, there aren't any rules about that," Harry said.

"Well, there should be."

Leeva put the thermos in her backpack next to Bob and strapped it onto her shoulders. It was heavier than when she'd walked in a few hours ago. The additional weight was not a burden, though, because it was the good solid heft of *having*.

RISKY KITTENS

Osmund was waiting on the sidewalk as usual. He didn't say anything about Leeva coming out through the front doors, and neither did she. Instead, she asked if he'd noticed any unusual activity on his way here. She asked it casually—the book she'd read last night had taught her some valuable detective skills.

"Unusual activity? Like what?"

"Oh, like, say, search parties. Police."

Osmund picked up Bob and clutched him tight. "What's happened?"

"Nothing, I was just wondering." She withdrew Harry's slip of paper and the map. "We have to get half a pound of cream cheese. At 222 Walnut Way. Let's go."

Bob, waddling between them, was always better

behaved with Osmund guiding him, and it occurred to Leeva that he might help with her other quest, too. "Osmund, what are people for?"

He answered without hesitation. "For insuring."

"Oh. But what does that mean?"

Osmund stopped. He fished out a business card from his pocket. "'Frisk Insurance,'" he read aloud. "'Bad things happen. Let us cushion the blow.'"

He handed the card to Leeva, and as they walked, Leeva pondered its message. The "bad things happen" part was true, she knew that, all right. Just last night, for instance, a very bad thing had happened indeed: She'd been forbidden to leave her property. It was comforting to imagine someone cushioning that terrible blow. *Would pillows have been involved?* she wondered.

Leeva slowed down as something remarkable struck her: She'd cushioned that blow herself, and without a single pillow. Although the old quilt had played a part.

Osmund was absolutely right. Protecting was something important that people were for. But she wondered about how it worked. "Can anyone insure anyone else?"

Osmund didn't answer. He had stopped in front of a shabby old house, lettered with the number 222. "Not going in there," he said with a shudder.

Leeva pocketed the business card and pulled out the slip of paper. "But this is it."

Osmund crossed his arms and raised his chin toward a sign—KITTENS!—taped to the door. "Claws, fleas, cat scratch fever. I could be allergic . . . too much risk." And then he plopped down on the curb and dragged Bob onto his lap.

Osmund's reaction worried Leeva a little. But Harry had sent her here, so she walked up to the door.

RISKY MILK

"I'm sorry I stayed so long," Leeva said when she came back outside. "I was having fun." As they walked, she told Osmund about her visit. "The people were nice. An old couple. And do they love their cats! They had a whole room just for them—screened, with lots of plants and tree branches nailed up across the whole room."

Osmund acted completely bored until Leeva showed him the collar the couple had given her. "Look, it has a pop-bead safety release. So Bob can't ever choke."

"Hmm . . . that's pretty good," he admitted as he took off the napkin ring and put the new collar around Bob's neck.

"They really love Harry, too. Harry gave them their first cat, about ten years ago. He was shoveling their

driveway, and they gave him some cocoa afterward and said how lonely they were with their kids all grown up, and so he brought them a kitten."

"That's Harry, all right," Osmund said. "He notices things and figures out a way to help."

"Well, the cats were all friendly," Leeva went on. "I bet they'd make good pets." She looked down at Bob. "Sorry, Bob. I didn't mean to hurt your feelings. And the kittens! Do you know about kittens, Osmund?"

Osmund shrugged.

"They're so funny! And their ears were so soft! You missed it all. For nothing."

Osmund hung his head.

"I think you must miss a lot of things," she said more kindly.

Osmund kept walking, but Leeva thought that maybe she saw him nod.

In the park, a pedestal had been erected at the scraped bare space. Bob ran over and began digging at its base, and Leeva and Osmund settled on a bench. Leeva handed Osmund his three cookies, then took out the thermos.

She unscrewed the cover, which she was delighted to see was also a cup. Leeva filled it and offered it to

Osmund, but he reared back. "Cow's milk. One point nine percent of children are allergic."

Leeva sniffed the milk. She took a cautious sip. It was creamy and cold, very nice. "It's too bad you have that allergy."

"Well, I don't *know* that I have it. It's too risky to try."

Leeva gaped at him. "You never even tried? All the things you miss out on—" She stopped. Osmund was turned away from her, but even under the shield she could see his face had purpled dangerously. She put down the thermos. "What's wrong?"

Osmund pointed to a sign on the tree. Statue Unveiling Ceremony—All Townspeople Ordered to Attend. "Those *Thornblossoms*," he practically spat. "Bob's an orphan because of their stupid statue, and now we're supposed to come here and watch it being unveiled?"

Even though she was upset, Leeva had to correct him. "It was *Mayor* Thornblossom who did this. I don't think Mr. Thornblossom was involved."

Osmund frowned. "He's awful, too. He takes everyone's money. It's an awful family. I bet their parents were awful." He paused, looking as if something had just struck him. "If they had kids, those kids would probably turn out awful, too."

"That's not fair," Leeva couldn't help saying. "Who says they'd all turn out the same?"

Osmund ignored her. "I don't think they have kids, though. At least, nobody in school has that name."

Leeva hadn't thought about this—in school, everyone would know her name, and who her parents were. Everyone in town seemed to despise them. She gathered her things, then walked over to Bob and scooped him up. "I have to get this cream cheese to Mrs. Flowers before it melts," she called over her shoulder in a wobbly voice. Then she took off before Osmund could follow.

All the way back to the library, though, she heard his words: *If they had kids, those kids would probably turn out awful, too.*

A PRESENT FOR HARRY

Leeva spent the rest of the afternoon reading in the library, trying not to think about what Osmund had said. When it closed, she left and circled the block until Harry emerged at five fifteen. "I'll walk with you to the park," she offered.

"Oh, good." Harry leaned over and plucked some cat hairs off her sleeve. "How was your adventure today?"

"It was great!" As they walked, Leeva told Harry everything that had happened. When they reached the park, she finished with the best thing. "The father cat, Mr. Cupcake, liked me so much he purred. Purring is how you know a cat is happy."

Leeva realized if she were a cat, she'd be purring, too—she was that happy. Except for one thing.

Finally, when they'd perched on the back of a bench, Leeva got to the question she wanted to ask. "Harry, if a person's parents did something wrong, something so bad it made other people angry, would that person . . ." She drew a deep breath. Asking her question was harder than she'd thought.

Harry put a hand over hers. "I knew you'd ask me about this," he said. "I was wondering when."

This surprised Leeva into silence.

"Of course, when I got old enough to learn what happened to my parents, I was upset. 'Really? Off to study hippopotamuses in the wild? When you have a little kid at home?'"

Leeva, remembering that sometimes what people were for was simply listening, nodded for him to go on.

"Well, my aunt wouldn't let me stay angry at them. She made sure

I knew my parents hadn't done anything bad or wrong. It was an accident: Sometimes a hippopotamus just doesn't feel like being studied. Does that answer your question?"

It did not, of course. But suddenly, Leeva no longer wanted to ask about her parents. Like a hippopotamus, she didn't feel like being studied. "That quilt in the book return," she asked instead. "Did it use to be yours?"

"How do you know about that quilt?"

Leeva gulped. She shouldn't have mentioned the quilt. "Um . . . you opened the book return for me once, remember?"

"Right, right." Harry nodded. "My mother had made it. Aunt Pauline made sure it came along when I came to live with her. I was very lucky, having someone like her in my life, and I know it. I owe her so much."

Sitting beside Harry, Leeva felt lucky, too. She owed him so much and she wished she had something to give him. And then she realized that she did. "Are you still looking for a girl for that part in the play?" she asked.

"We are. It's such a small part, we're using a manne-quin. A stagehand hides behind it and reads the lines.

But it would be great to have a real girl. I'm glad you changed your mind."

"Not me. You know Fern, with all the little brothers and sisters?" Leeva ignored the sudden cold pinch of jealousy. "She's very dramatic."

Harry considered. "You're right. I bet she'd be great. Tell her to stop in to the Community Theater, see the director." He looked up at the town clock. "Well, it's time." And then he left, whistling.

Leeva ducked into the bathrooms and stayed there until she felt sure her parents would have left the Town Hall. Somehow they hadn't noticed she was missing this morning, but when they got back this evening they'd be sure to find out when they saw the unsolved bookkeeping problem and the dirty dishes. She would have to be extra careful now.

"We'll stick to the back roads again," she told Bob as she leashed him up. "We can take as much time as you want."

Bob took advantage of this and snuffled at everything that could possibly be of interest. As it grew dark, lights began turning on in the houses. Leeva stopped now and then to watch families in kitchens, making meals together. The sight made her stomach feel empty. Or maybe it was a spot a little above her stomach.

When it was fully dark, Leeva returned to the library.

Lights glowed only on the third floor, so she changed into her pajamas, washed out the clothes she'd been wearing at the faucet, and hung them to dry deep in the hedge. She was tired from the day, but she did her exercises from *Vim and Vigor*.

There was only one more thing to do before she could settle in for the night. She leashed Bob to the book drop and very, *very* cautiously pushed through the hedge into her own backyard.

For a moment, she stood, listening. Hearing nothing, she tiptoed around front.

There sat her parents' car all by itself—no police cruiser beside it, no search dogs, no detectives poring over clues.

Through the big living room picture window, she saw that both televisions were on. Silhouetted in their blue glow were two figures, one tall and pointed, one short and round. The figures were seated and looked relaxed. They were not weeping wretchedly, not running about frantically, ripping the room apart or shouting into phones.

Leeva had her answer. Her parents had to know by now that she was gone, and they weren't going to look for her.

She was quite relieved by this, of course. She certainly did not want to be found. And she shouldn't be surprised, she told herself. After all, her parents told her often enough to stop talking and go away—now that she'd done just that, why would they go looking for her? Yes, she was relieved.

And yet, looking into the living room made her throat hurt.

Leeva turned away. She scrambled through the hedge back to the book drop. "We're safe," she whispered to Bob as she untied him. "That's what matters."

Then she climbed into the book drop. She kept Bob occupied until she heard Harry come whistling up the drive from his rehearsal, then let him out for the night.

There were at least twenty books in the return this night, and they all looked good. Leeva flipped through a karate magazine and skimmed a picture book about bees while she ate the six remaining cookies and drank the rest of the cool milk.

Then she picked up a how-to book called *Living Big in Your Tiny House*. Although none of the tips would help—*Hang mirrors! Take the doors off! Paint the walls a light color!*—the book was encouraging. *That's what I'll do*, she thought sleepily: *Live big in my tiny house.*

THE STANDOFF

Reader, remember how happy Leeva thought she was just the week before? Well, that was nothing compared to the joy she felt living big in that book drop.

Each morning, she woke early. After erasing all traces of her stay, she visited the Nutsmore Public Park bathroom. Next it was back to the library, where she greeted patrons and helped out until noon, when she shared a delicious lunch with Harry and his aunt on the stoop.

After lunch, Osmund always tagged along on her ingredient-fetching, and afterward they always brought Bob to the park. When Osmund left, Leeva headed to Fern's.

Right from the start, this was her favorite part of the day.

Yes, it was loud there—seven little boys and girls shrieking and laughing—but it was a happy clamor, and so it made Leeva feel happy, too. And yes, there was a lot to do—watching over those seven little kids and two old people—but Fern explained that it made her feel proud to help her parents.

This made Leeva consider. She'd never really tried to get her parents what they wanted, but now that she was out, maybe she should. She wouldn't mind feeling proud. Asking this family for money for her father was out of the question, but perhaps she could make her mother more famous.

"Have you ever noticed what high hair Mayor Thornblossom has?" she asked in the most admiring tone she could muster.

The two extremely old people woke up at that, their eyes bulging alarmingly. Fern fell off her chair laughing. "High hair?" she repeated from the floor, lifting her single braid straight up. "*High hair?* You're so funny, Leeva."

Oh, well, she'd tried.

The best part of visiting Fern was when *Vim and*

Vigor was on. Once everyone was jumping around in front of the television, Leeva and Fern escaped to the porch to drape themselves over chaise lounges and talk about books.

Talking about books you'd both read was like talking about people you both knew, things you'd both done. Leeva and Fern had read so many of the same books, they felt they'd grown up together.

"I'm usually shy," Fern noted as they were discussing *Where the Red Fern Grows*, "but with you I'm not." As if to prove it, she stood up and acted out the scene at the dogs' grave so compellingly, she and Leeva both cried real tears.

Anyone could see that Fern would be a sensation on a stage. Leeva wiped her cheeks. The time had come. "You know, Harry's in a play at the Community Theater," she began, and this time she felt only the tiniest pinch in her heart. "He said they're looking for a girl to be in it. I told him about you."

"I *wish*. But . . ." Fern grew pale. "But no. All those people, looking at me. Oh, no, I couldn't."

"That's called stage fright. Harry said he knows a trick to help."

Fern said, "Maybe," but she didn't look convinced.

Each evening, when Fern's family got home, Leeva said goodbye and wandered through her town thinking her own thoughts in peace, which felt like a luxury. And then each night, back in the book return, she enjoyed six cookies and the rest of the cold milk, reading by the light of her headlamp.

Reader, after three of these perfect days, Leeva grew dangerously careless.

On that fourth morning, she practically sashayed up the library steps. As she walked inside, she actually opened her mouth to call out, "I'm here!"

What she saw at the desk, though, froze the words on her tongue, and it was a good thing they did.

Dead ahead of her, a woman was looming over the librarian on five-inch stilettos, her hair stacked in a threatening tower.

Leeva dove behind an armchair, her heart hammering. She slipped off her backpack and wriggled under the chair.

Leeva's mother thrust a paper at Mrs. Flowers. "Put this up."

Mrs. Flowers read the paper, then thrust it back. "No. Our notice board is only for announcements of importance to the community."

"My statue unveiling is of the *utmost* importance to the community. Everyone has to be there, or else. It's an order. Put it up beside my portrait." Mayor Thornblossom spun around, scanning the walls. "Where *is* my portrait?"

Mrs. Flowers nodded toward the clutter at the back door, to the large draped piece that Leeva had hidden behind the first day she'd entered the library. "We needed space for books. This is a library."

"This is a public building. All public buildings must put up my portrait." An ominous scritching accompanied the words.

Put up the portrait, Leeva begged Mrs. Flowers silently. *Just do it*.

Mrs. Flowers did not. "I can't waste the space."

Leeva's mother clicked over to the elevator. "Put it up on this silver wall." She swanned her head at her reflection in its mirrory finish. "Yes, here. What is this, anyway?"

Mrs. Flowers seemed to grow taller. "That's an elevator. It is essential. Without it, many of our patrons can't access the second floor. Without it, I can't do my job."

Scritch-scritch-scritch. "Well, your job is to put up my portrait and this notice."

Please, please, please say you'll do it, Leeva wished harder.

But Mrs. Flowers held firm. "As I've explained before, I don't work for you," she growled. Her earrings flashed. "I work for the people of Nutsmore. And so do you."

Well, Reader, that put a fork in it! Leeva's mother ground a heel so violently it snapped completely off. You could practically see the fury steaming out of her ears as she stomp-hobbled out.

The punishment was going to be horrible.

For two days, Leeva stayed close to the library, keeping a nervous watch, although for what she didn't know. For two days, nothing happened.

Perhaps her mother was distracted by the preparations for the statue unveiling—Leeva had noticed a lot of activity at the site, workers measuring and carting in materials. "Now she wants the pedestal taller," complained one builder. "Says she wants people to look up to her." "She fired the sculptor yesterday," said another. "She fired me, twice!"

Yes, that was probably it: In the heaven of bossing people around, Mayor Thornblossom had probably forgotten about punishing the librarian.

Leeva was wrong, of course. Horribly, dreadfully wrong.

TOAST, GLORIOUS TOAST

On the third day, Leeva emerged from the book drop to find a rainbow overhead—a quick shower had awakened her—that seemed to promise a lucky day. Things in the library seemed just fine, except that Harry didn't come out to the stoop for lunch. "He's still upstairs revising his play. Trouble with the dialogue," Mrs. Flowers said, setting the lunch tray down. "We'll start without him."

Lunch looked good, but Leeva noticed that Mrs. Flowers didn't take any of it. Instead, on her plate was a single slice of bread, cut in half.

Leeva leaned over. Actually, the thing on Pauline Flowers's plate looked like a slice of bread, but it was darker and somehow looked stiffer. And the *fragrance*!

"What *is* that?"

Mrs. Flowers chuckled. "Too much cookie dough this morning, I'm afraid. I'm giving my stomach a rest." She picked up one half of the mysterious bread-shaped food and took a bite. The mysterious bread-shaped food made a crunch.

"But what *is* it?" Leeva asked again, sniffing deeply.

Mrs. Flowers stopped, her hand midway to her lips, bracelets jangling. "You don't know *toast?*"

"That's toast? I've read about it and always wondered."

Mrs. Flowers's mouth fell open. She handed Leeva the plate with the other half of the toast on it.

Leeva picked up the toast. The scent, wafting up this close, nearly made her swoon.

She took a bite. *Crunch!* Her eyes closed in ecstasy.

She took another bite, sighing in bliss. And another and another. The taste was beyond deluxe. As she swallowed the last morsel, she opened her eyes, half-surprised to find she was still on earth. And then she glanced up.

Tears were rolling down Pauline Flowers's cheeks.

"What's wrong?" Leeva cried.

"Nothing, nothing," Mrs. Flowers assured her, dabbing her tears with her scarf. "It's just that . . . Most people, they don't appreciate toast. Too simple, I guess. Too common. But you've got it right." Her face clouded over. "For a child to have been denied this comforting nourishment is simply inexcusable." She growled and rose from her chair.

Leeva got up, too, but Mrs. Flowers put out a hand. "No. You stay right here." And she went inside.

Leeva heard the elevator whoosh up and then a minute later, whoosh down. Mrs. Flowers emerged carrying another tray. On it was an entire loaf of bread, a knife, a stick of butter, and a sleek metal box with two slots in its rounded top and a cord trailing from its base. "This is a toaster," she said.

Mrs. Flowers set everything on the little table and plugged the toaster into an outlet Leeva had never noticed. "Take two slices from the loaf," she instructed.

Leeva obeyed. The bread was pale and soft. It smelled good, but not divine. At Mrs. Flowers's direction, she placed a slice in each slot, and then pressed down a bar.

The bread disappeared. The divine scent began to curl up from the glowing slots. Second by second it intensified, until the slices popped back up, toasted to a golden brown.

"Now, the butter," Mrs. Flowers said, cutting a pat

with the knife, "is all about timing. Some folks like to butter their toast while it's hot, so the butter melts in completely. Some people—toast-warm, butter-cold folks—wait several seconds. You can experiment." She handed Leeva the knife and the plate.

The butter softened as Leeva spread it. When every square inch was covered, she gobbled both slices, unable to speak for her pleasure.

When she was finished, Mrs. Flowers nodded toward the loaf. "Make as much as you like. I'll go brew some tea and see if Harry wants me to read over his lines."

When Mrs. Flowers left, Leeva put another two slices into the magical toaster. As it heated up, she noticed voices coming from inside the library. How odd—Mrs. Flowers had never before opened the library during lunch.

The toaster glowed, and so did Leeva. Finally, someone had taken her side. Mrs. Flowers had called her parents' behavior inexcusable. Now here she was making *toast*—as much as she liked! "Bob," she said, "today is going to be the best day of my life." Bob, curled up in a pot of oregano, didn't wake up.

The toast popped up. Leeva buttered it. It was even

better than before. She put another two slices in.

While it cooked, she heard more voices inside. She buttered her toast and took her time eating it. She put another two slices in and ate them slowly, savoring each morsel. As she was about to take a final bite, she heard a blistering crack.

She dropped the toast. Inside, on the top floor, Harry was revising a play and his aunt was brewing tea. Neither activity should produce a sound like that.

Then came the screech of cleaved metal. Next, Leeva heard Harry cry out, "Stop! Stop!"

The cracking and screeching did not stop. And then came the worst sound she had ever heard in her life: Pauline Flowers sobbing, *"No, no, no!"* as if her heart were being cut out.

Leeva charged inside.

STOLEN!

The place was a wreck. Books had been knocked from shelves, armchairs overturned, and the two large front doors hung crookedly from their hinges.

"Mrs. Flowers! Harry! Where are you? Are you all right?" A chunk of plaster fell at Leeva's feet.

She looked up. There was a huge, ragged hole in the ceiling of the nonfiction floor. Through it she could see right into the apartment.

Only then did she realize—the elevator had been removed!

Mrs. Flowers peered over the edge of the hole. "We're coming down. Stay right where you are."

Harry appeared by her side, ashen-faced. He picked

her up and navigated the tricky spiral stairway, carrying her as if she were a large, fragile egg, and set her down at the bottom. "Ten men . . . with axes . . ." His gaze was glassy, his pupils huge.

Luckily, as the Clevertons routinely went into shock, Leeva recognized the symptoms. "Lie down," she ordered. Then she lifted his feet onto a stool to keep the blood in his head.

"Well done, Leeva," Mrs. Flowers said. Then her expression turned fierce.

She and Leeva dashed to the doorway. What looked like a giant, silver, twenty-legged caterpillar hovered at the end of the walkway. As it turned onto the sidewalk,

Leeva could see that the twenty legs belonged to ten men carrying the elevator on their backs.

"Stop, thieves!" Mrs. Flowers yelled. Then she bent low as if she was trying to see under the elevator. "Why, Robbie Flamble! Is that you?"

One of the men ducked his head out. "Yes, ma'am."

"And little Mario Junior? And Lefty Sluggins?"

One by one, all ten men answered sheepishly when she called their names.

"I've known you since you were little boys. And now you've all become thieves?"

The one called Robbie Flamble said, "We're not thieves, Mrs. Flowers. We're just following orders."

"Orders? Whose orders?" Mrs. Flowers demanded.

Leeva knew. She knew the answer before Robbie Flamble said it.

"Mayor Thornblossom's, ma'am."

Harry staggered over then. He put his arm around his aunt, who slumped against his shoulder. They gaped as the elevator for which he had given up his heart's desire so that she could regain hers disappeared down the sidewalk.

The expressions on their faces hurt Leeva in a way she'd never been hurt before. She dashed past them and ran after the stolen elevator.

It didn't go far.

It stopped at Leeva's driveway. Then it turned. Leeva followed and watched in horror as the ten men carried the elevator right up to her house and then slid it in through the big picture window.

SOMETHING AWFUL

Leeva walked back to the library, feeling as if each foot weighed a hundred pounds. As she approached, she heard the *swish, swish, swish* of a broom and the *thunk, thunk, thunk* of books being placed on shelves. She dragged herself up the wide front steps and stood rooted for a moment, clutching the library card at her neck. Then she stepped inside.

Harry stopped sweeping and his aunt put down the book she was holding.

Leeva braced herself. "My parents took your elevator. Mayor Thornblossom is my mother. Treasurer Thornblossom is my father. I'm a Thornblossom."

"Uh-huh," Mrs. Flowers said, shelving another book.

Harry started sweeping again.

"Aren't you surprised? Did you already know?"

Mrs. Flowers looked insulted. "Of *course* I knew," she exclaimed, hands on her hips. "I'm a *librarian!*"

"But how?" Leeva asked. "When?"

"I was standing at the kitchen window upstairs when you came through the hedge that first day. I thought, *now that's going to be interesting*. And I was right." She went back to her shelving.

"Harry?"

Harry shrugged. "Sure I knew. I'm a librarian's nephew."

Leeva was flabbergasted. She had a lot more to ask, but just then, Osmund came into view. During the past horrible hour—had it only been an hour?—Leeva had completely forgotten.

He leaned in the doorway. He yanked up his face shield. His eyes popped. "What happened?"

Harry slid a reassuring glance Leeva's way. "Our elevator has been removed, Osmund," he said carefully.

"Mayor Thornblossom took it," Mrs. Flowers added quickly. "That's who's to blame, and no one else. Now, I need peppermint sprinkles for tomorrow's recipe. Harry, where should she go for them?"

Harry went to the desk and scribbled on a slip of

paper. He gave it to Leeva.

"No, we'll stay and help you clean up," she offered.

"Later," Mrs. Flowers said firmly. "Right now, getting those sprinkles is more important. Because if I don't bake Coco-Mint Pinwheels tomorrow, Mayor Thornblossom has won."

Harry went upstairs and got Leeva's tin of cookies and thermos of milk, as if it was a normal day.

Leeva gathered Bob, who was still asleep in the oregano. She sealed up the bread and brought in the toaster, then she walked away with Osmund as if it was a normal day, too.

But it wasn't. Something awful had happened. All the way to get the peppermint sprinkles, then all the way to the park, and all the way back, Leeva felt terrible. The only comfort she could take was that Harry and his aunt had known who she was all along, and it hadn't mattered to them.

HUGGED

When Leeva got back to the library, the big front doors were hung on their hinges properly, but they were locked.

She walked around the building and found Harry sitting on the stoop, his arms wrapped around his knees, papers scattered beside him. She nestled Bob back into the oregano plant and sat beside Harry. The papers were his play, she saw. "Are you having trouble with your dialogue again?"

"I wish." Harry squeezed his eyes shut and shook his head. "I have to quit my classes, Leeva."

"Why, Harry?" Leeva gasped.

He flapped a hand behind him. "Those stairs, remember? Aunt Pauline can't manage them and I can't carry her up and down all day. She'll be stuck in the apartment again. And I'll be . . ." He buried his face in his hands.

Leeva slumped as if someone had dropped a lead blanket over her shoulders. Of course: Without the elevator, Harry would have to take over for his aunt again. He'd have to follow in her footsteps and do all the things he said he was happy to do, but wasn't.

Maybe Osmund was right. Maybe people did end up just like their parents—or aunt—no matter how much they didn't want to.

Suddenly, she had a question to ask. An urgent, but dangerous, question. She swallowed and swallowed, until finally she could get it out. "Harry, do children always turn out like the people who raised them? Do they always do the same things?"

He raised both hands and pointed down at himself, as if to say, *Yes, here's proof.* He really was a good actor.

"But do they *have* to?"

"Well, I feel it's my duty. I owe her so much. And really, I'm glad I can—" And then he stopped. He looked at Leeva so kindly it felt as if he were patting her shoulder with his eyes. "Oh," he said. "You're not talking about me, are you."

Leeva shook her head. Her eyes stung. She stared straight forward and clutched her knees.

"Would you like a hug?" Harry Flowers asked.

Hugs had been in a great many of the books Leeva had read. The characters on *The Winds of Our Tides* seemed to enjoy them. Everyone in Fern's family seemed to love them. "Yes, I think so. I think I'd like to try one."

Harry wrapped his arms around her and squeezed just the perfect amount. Then he let go. "Was that all right?"

"Yes. I liked your hug very much," she said. "Could you do it again?"

Harry could. He did.

"Do you think your aunt would do it?"

"Oh, I'm pretty sure she would. I'll go up and carry her down."

When he was gone, Leeva quickly gathered his pages. If Mrs. Flowers saw them, she would feel sad. Besides, maybe someday Harry would want them again. She would insure him against that possible loss. She slid them into her backpack. Then she went inside.

"Would you hug me, please, Mrs. Flowers?" she asked when Harry brought her down.

"Oh, my, yes," Mrs. Flowers said. "I've been wanting

to do that for quite a while now."

Harry's aunt's hug smelled like vanilla and baked sugar, and it felt the way cookies would feel if they were made into a coat.

"May I be hugged while you answer my question, Harry?" Leeva asked.

"What question?" asked Harry.

"Children. Do they always turn out like their parents?"

"Oh, right. Good plan."

Mrs. Flowers sat on an armchair and patted her lap. Leeva climbed on. She had never sat on anyone's lap before, and she found it surprisingly nice. The lap was commodious.

Mrs. Flowers wrapped her arms around Leeva. "This is a backward hug, but it's still a hug," she assured her. "And I won't let go."

Leeva clasped her hands over Mrs. Flowers's hands just in case.

Harry stood in front of them. He cleared his throat and lifted his chin. Immediately, he looked Harry-er. He pressed one hand to his heart and flung the other toward the ceiling. "We ourselves, not the stars, hold our destiny!" he began in a deep voice.

And then Harry really got cranking. "Fear not the fickle storms of fate!" he cried. "Welcome instead the steady currents of your soul!" His voice rose as he went on, until the words reverberated like thunderbolts. It made Leeva want to stand up and cheer. "Take thou thine clay," he roared, "and sculpt from it a stairway to reach thine dreams—"

Just then the telephone rang and Harry dashed to answer it.

Leeva turned to face Mrs. Flowers. "I don't know what he was talking about," she confided. "But I really liked how he was saying it!"

Mrs. Flowers chuckled. "Yes, that boy belongs on a stage. Now, I think what he was trying to tell you was this: *no.* Children do not have to turn out like their parents, do the same things they did. If they want to, they may. If not, they can decide not to."

"Really?" Leeva asked.

"Really. Now there are some things you get from your family that you can't change. Red hair, big ears, tall or short—that kind of thing. But those are only . . . body parts. They do not determine how you travel through life, or where you go."

"So . . . what your parents give you is like a car."

"Yes, exactly! Maybe you can't change some things about this car. But you don't have to drive it where your parents did. You may drive it alone, or fill it with friends. You may have grand adventures or quiet wanders in this car. You may run noble errands, or simply zip around for the fun of seeing what's around the next corner. You will explore this whole beautiful world in your car, Leeva, and be anyone you want inside it."

As Leeva thought about this, she felt something strange happening to her face.

Just then Harry came back. "Oh, it's so nice to see you smile, Leeva!" he said. "What are you thinking?"

"I was thinking I'm glad I have a car, Harry," Leeva answered, climbing down from Mrs. Flowers's lap. "I have a lot of places to go."

THE PUDDLE

Thoughts about that car encouraged Leeva all the next day. Even watching Bob dig in the park didn't depress her as much: No, she did *not* have to turn into the kind of person who would destroy a badger's home just to put up a statue of herself.

While Osmund tweezed cookie crumbs out of his face mask and gloves, Leeva got up to investigate something glinting on a walkway.

The something turned out to be a puddle. Leeva's driveway was gravel, her yard all weeds, so she'd never seen one before.

She knelt beside it. There was her own face reflected against a background of blue sky and white clouds, as if she were floating . . . ha! When a bird flew overhead and seemed to disappear into her ear, she laughed out loud. It all seemed to suggest that Mrs. Flowers was right: She could be anyone she wanted, even a floating girl with birds in her head.

Osmund ran over. "Get away! People can drown in two inches of water!"

"Well, maybe. But I won't." Leeva trailed her fingers through the cool water. "It feels so silky. And look, my face is rippling!"

"There could be broken glass on the bottom! Also, germs! Also, bacteria!"

Leeva peeled off her sandals and stuck her feet into the cool water.

"Mosquito larvae! Parasites!"

"Osmund, stop." She plopped in an acorn.

"Rat bites! Rats love water! Bad things happen, Leeva!"

"Good things happen, too, Osmund!" Leeva shouted. She sighed. It was clear where Osmund had gotten his dismal point of view. Pondering this, she had an idea. She pulled her feet out so Osmund could calm down, and then she began. "You know, what you get from your parents is like a car."

"They wouldn't give me a car. They don't even own one."

Leeva tried again. "No. What your parents give you is *like* a car. And you don't have to—"

"We have a golf cart instead. It's *like* a car, but a whole lot safer. Injury from crashes is directly proportional to speed at impact. For example . . ."

Osmund began a recitation of accident statistics so depressing that Leeva had to tape her sandals back on and walk away.

But Osmund followed her and kept at it as they walked out of the park. Even when they reached his doorstep and he patted Bob goodbye, he still wasn't finished. "And without seat belts, riders sustain much more serious injuries."

Leeva felt as if she herself had sustained a serious injury from Osmund's lecture. She understood now why he didn't have any friends. Oddly, Osmund himself seemed pretty miserable from the whole thing, too. She didn't point this out, though—who was she to give anyone advice?

LEEVA THE EMBEZZLER

ack at the library that afternoon, Leeva found Harry shoving a tall bookcase across the room. "Lots to do," he panted, "so we can reopen tomorrow."

Mrs. Flowers was downstairs, too. "A little more to the left," she directed from the armchair. She motioned to a bunch of boxes. "The cookbooks. But first, Leeva, will you help shelve the town reports upstairs with me?"

Leeva put down her pack, with Bob snoring inside, and followed as Harry carried his aunt upstairs. It was obviously a lot harder than carrying her down.

The floor up there had been repaired and the bookcase was already in place. A dozen boxes surrounded it.

Leeva sat on the floor and slid one over to her side.

Mrs. Flowers picked up a rag and began to dust the shelves. "Most folks think cookbooks belong up here. I understand, but there are plenty of stories in a good meal, too, don't you think?"

"Mm-hmm . . ." Leeva opened the box. It was full of thick blue ledgers. Curious, she pulled one out and began scanning the columns.

Harry was right, the town reports were boring—no plot! no characters!—but she did not find the numbers hard to understand. "So the year before last, at least," she said, "you had plenty of money in the library budget. You could have bought an elevator. Dozens of elevators."

Mrs. Flowers frowned. "What year was that?"

Leeva held up the ledger, spine out, to show her.

"No, certainly not. There's been no money in the budget for three years." She shot a glance out the window facing Leeva's house so quick that most people would not have noticed it.

But Leeva was not most people. She noticed the glance. She knew what it meant. But at that moment, she had something more pressing on her mind. "But it says here, 'Four hundred ninety-nine thousand, six hundred eleven dollars to the Nutsmore Public Library.'"

Mrs. Flowers dropped her dustcloth. She folded her arms. "That's just not true."

Leeva got up and brought over the ledger so she might see for herself.

Mrs. Flowers held up a palm. "No, I trust you." She looked as if she was thinking hard. "Would you check last year?"

Leeva shuffled through the ledgers for the right one. "You received three hundred twenty-eight thousand, six hundred forty dollars."

"We surely did not. What about the schools? Does it say they got any money?"

Leeva checked. "One million, even, to each, elementary, middle, and high school."

Harry poked his head up from the spiral staircase. Apparently he'd been listening. "The Community Theater?"

Leeva checked. "Two hundred thousand, fifty."

Understanding hit her like a plank. She staggered.

Mrs. Flowers and Harry seemed to understand also.

They stared at her with a mix of emotions Leeva had never seen on *The Winds of Our Tides*.

Pauline Flowers was the one who finally spoke the words. "Your father embezzled the money from the town."

"He cooked the books," Harry confirmed.

"Cooked the books?" Leeva asked.

"Cheated, by using shady accounting."

Leeva stared at the criminal evidence.

And then another plank of understanding whacked her. $499,611. $328,640. $1,000,000. $200,050.

Leeva recognized those numbers.

She collapsed onto the floor. She lay there, numb with horror.

Mrs. Flowers hurried over. "Dear girl, of course it's a shock to learn that your father is a criminal."

"It's worse than that," Leeva managed to croak. "My father didn't cook the books."

"I'm afraid he did. This is proof."

"No." Leeva sat up. She drew a shaky breath. "*He* didn't." She covered her face with her hands. "*I* did."

GREENISH PAPER?

"Every day! Every single day for over three years I solved the bookkeeping problems my father left! And he always made me sign them—now I know why." Leeva kept her face buried in her hands. "*I'm* the criminal!"

Leeva heard two gasps. She peeked out through her fingers.

Harry and his aunt stepped toward her, arms opened.

Leeva jumped up and clattered down the stairs. Criminals didn't deserve hugs. She snatched her pack and fled through the back door, running so hard her braids lifted, and crashed through the hedge to hide in her own yard.

Bob woke at that and started scratching to get out.

Leeva set him at the base of an old oak—her parents wouldn't be back for an hour at least. "I'm going to prison," she told him.

Bob took the news well—he began snuffling around the roots—but Leeva began to shake.

She sank down, grateful to feel the solid trunk at her spine. She knew what prison was like. On the last episode of *The Winds of Our Tides* that she'd seen, Mr. and Mrs. Cleverton had gotten locked up for a crime actually committed by evil impostors. Oh, the anguish as they were dragged off. Oh, the loneliness and menace in those dark, bare cells!

Just remembering it made Leeva feel as if someone had scraped out her insides with a grapefruit spoon. She wished she could run back and say, *Yes, please* to those hugs Harry and his aunt had offered.

She wouldn't, though. Harry and his aunt had enough sadness right now—sadness she herself had caused by her criminal arithmetic!—without taking on any more.

Leeva wrapped her own arms around herself. Although it didn't help the scraped-out feeling, it did stop the shaking.

It was time to brace up and face this disaster. Yes,

she was responsible for it. But didn't that just mean she was responsible for fixing things? "You are vimful and vigorous," she told herself in as inspiring a tone as she could muster. "You can do it."

Bob peered around the tree. "You are vimful and vigorous, too," she told him, patting his head. "You can do it, too." Everyone could use a little encouragement, after all.

She crossed her legs, propped her chin on her hands, and got to work.

What had to happen was simple: The stolen money must be returned. But her father certainly wasn't going to give it back, even though he had said himself that he would never do anything with it.

When he'd told her that, Leeva remembered, she'd pointed out, "But then it's just boxes of greenish paper."

Boxes of greenish paper. There was an idea hiding in that phrase. She lifted her gaze to her house. Those boxes of greenish paper were right up there on the top floor. Suddenly Leeva remembered the coincidence that had struck her when she'd been making Bob his leash. The top floor was full of greenish paper, while the basement was full of grayish paper.

A plan began to hatch. What if she could simply

make a switch: Fill the shoeboxes upstairs with the newspapers from down in the basement? Her father would still have his full boxes, and she could give back the money.

How *perfect*.

Well, not quite. There were two problems.

The first was the color. Her father had definitely said he wanted boxes full of *greenish* paper. This could not be ignored.

Leeva pulled Bob onto her lap. As she picked leaves out of his fur, she searched her mind for anything she might have that could color them green. *Paint? No. Markers? No.*

She stroked Bob's ears. They were not as soft as those kittens' ears, but they were very nice. *Chalk? No.*

She rubbed his belly, the way the kittens had liked. *Stain?*

Stain. She'd heard that word recently. Leeva put Bob down. She sat perfectly still—memories could be shy—until it came to her: When she'd leaned over the pot of green dandelion stew, Fern had warned, "Careful, it stains."

THE CONFESSION

Leeva worked with Harry all the next morning, tidying the last shelves and corners until you couldn't tell there had ever been an elevator in the library, never mind one that had been ripped out. Which made her want to weep.

When they opened the doors at nine, loads of people pressed in—they'd missed their library the past few days. Leeva ran up and down the treacherous stairs fetching books, while Harry manned the checkout desk. Every few minutes there came a growl or a crash from the top floor.

At lunch on the stoop, she made a vow to Harry. "I'm going to make it up to you. And to the whole town."

Mrs. Flowers leaned out the window. "Don't be

ridiculous," she yelled down, waving a sandwich. "It's not your fault."

"I signed my name on every amount that was stolen. I didn't mean for it to be stolen, but I did the accounting," Leeva said firmly. "That means it's up to me to fix it."

After lunch, Leeva stood stock-still at the end of the library's walkway with Osmund beside her. In her hand was the slip of paper Harry had just given her. On it was written *48 orange jelly beans* and the address where the jelly beans would be found. She knew exactly where this address was, yet she didn't move. She had a decision to make and it involved taking a risk. *People are unpredictable*, she could almost hear Osmund warning.

Osmund picked up Bob. "Pecan Place, number forty-seven," he read over her shoulder. He pointed east. "Let's go."

Leeva made her decision. Instead of turning east, she turned west. She walked along the front hedge of her house until she reached the driveway. She closed her eyes and took an enormous breath. And then she started walking.

"Stop!" Osmund screamed, yanking her back. "That's the Thornblossoms' house!"

Leeva shook her arm free. "It is my house, also," she declared. "My name is Leeva Thornblossom."

Osmund stared at her, mouth agape.

"I am a Thornblossom," Leeva said. "And I need your help."

Osmund goggled at her some more and then turned back toward the library.

Leeva read his thoughts as clearly as if they were printed across his face shield. "Yes, the Flowerses know who I am," she said. "And they trust me." Then she closed her eyes again. She did not say another word.

After an excruciating moment, Leeva felt Osmund take her hand. People were unpredictable, all right.

And something warm and powerful, something that was the opposite of the scraped-out-with-a-grapefruit-spoon feeling, something that was more like a filled-up-with-a-soup-ladle feeling, flowed in to her hand, right through Osmund's Level C gloves. Apparently Friendship was not a hazardous material.

Together, they marched up to the doorstep. Leeva parted the briars and they went in.

Osmund gasped when he saw the stolen elevator. Bob hissed.

Leeva didn't want to get into it, but the stairs had

been removed, so what else could she do? She opened the door and waved Osmund inside. She pressed the Down button and led him into the basement storeroom.

There, she explained her plan.

"Your father really won't care?"

"Not as long as he has his boxes full of greenish paper. We'll start collecting dandelions this afternoon. I'll go get some grocery bags."

Osmund nodded gravely. "We're going to need a lot. And you're going to need a suit."

THE SMOKING GLARE

Osmund had muttered about all the problems they might encounter the whole way to get the jelly beans—Leeva had insisted they do that first—and Leeva had ignored him. But now, knuckles raised to Fern's door, she spared him a glance over her shoulder.

His hazmat suit was trembling and the bag of jelly beans was alarmingly mashed.

Leeva rescued the jelly bean bag. "Osmund," she asked in a soothing voice, "what are the odds of something bad happening when you knock on a door?"

"It's dangerous! Point zero zero two six that the door itself will fall on you!"

Leeva had only asked the question because she knew what a calming effect quoting doomful probabilities had on Osmund. But just then an idea occurred to her. "So . . . that means the odds of the door *not* falling on you are ninety-nine point nine nine seven four. Right?"

Osmund scratched at his hood as he checked the math. "Well . . . I guess," he agreed. "But—"

"And what about the odds of something *good* happening from knocking on a door . . . Do you know what they are?"

"Insurance isn't about *good* things that happen."

Leeva ignored his scornful tone. She was on to something. "Well, something good *could* happen from knocking on a door, correct?"

Osmund hesitated, as if he was trying to find a trick in Leeva's question, then nodded reluctantly. "But there are lots of other people in there," he whimpered. "People are the most dangerous. I *told* you."

Suddenly Leeva pictured his SafetyLand table. Both times she'd seen it, the animals had been gathered tightly around Osmundio, as if they really liked him.

"Osmund?" she asked gently. "Are you worried that someone in there won't like you?"

He dropped his head.

"But what if one of them *does* like you?"

"What if they *don't*, though?" he whispered.

"I'm kind of new to meeting people," she ventured, "but I wonder: Maybe if you don't try to scare them with every awful thing that might happen . . ." She turned back to the door before he could argue. "Anyway, there's only one way to find out." And with that, she knocked.

Fern answered. Her eyes narrowed when she saw Osmund.

"Osmund, this is my friend Fern," Leeva announced quickly. "Fern, meet Osmund. He's my friend, too."

Osmund nodded. "The bracken fern is poisonous. It can cause blindness and hemorrhaging."

Fern shrank back.

Leeva spun to face Osmund. Of the many meaningful looks on *The Winds of Our Tides*, none was more effective than the smoking glare. She'd never given anyone a smoking glare before, but now she screwed up her eyes and let one fly.

The glare did the trick. Osmund gulped and jumped back. "The odds of that happening are very low, though," he mumbled.

Leeva dialed the glare up a notch. He needed to do better.

"Actually," Osmund offered, "ferns are among the least dangerous plants in the world. So it's a good, safe name."

Fern stepped out onto the porch, although she kept a wary eye trained on Osmund. Then she did something surprising: She closed the door.

"You don't have to watch everybody?"

"Not anymore," Fern said, sweeping the thought away with a dramatic wave of languor. "My great-grandparents have gotten so vimful and vigorous they take care of my brothers and sisters. I'm a lady of leisure now. What's your mission?"

"That green stuff on your stove the other day," Leeva said, getting down to business. "You said it stains?"

"Dandelion stew. Anything it touches."

"Dandelion stew," Leeva repeated firmly. "We have to make a lot."

BOB TO THE RESCUE

Leeva passed out the bags. "So. Dandelions," she said once the three of them reached the street. "Where do we get them?"

Fern pointed down. Beside her foot was a flat crown of jagged leaves. "Dandelion." She pointed to patch after patch of green splattered over the sidewalk. "And that, and that, and that."

"Those are dandelions? I've seen them everywhere." Leeva crouched. "They grow through cracks in the concrete." She brushed her fingers over the plants. How heroic they were, persisting in growing against such odds, with no one caring for them. "I never really looked at them before."

She dropped to her knees beside one in bloom. As

she stroked it in appreciation, Osmund reached a finger down, too.

"We'll leave the ones with the flowers alone," Leeva decided. And then she realized something. "Osmund! No gloves?"

Osmund looked down at his bare hands, as if seeing them were a surprise to him, too. "Well, yesterday you said the puddle water felt silky . . . And just now . . ."

Leeva, remembering that sometimes *nothing* is exactly what someone likes to hear, said exactly that.

In the few short blocks to the park entrance, they filled half of their grocery bags with dandelion greens. But Leeva noticed that Fern never said a word to Osmund, and he never spoke to her. Fern was tongue-tied by shyness, and Osmund by fear.

Leeva left them alone together with Bob while she visited the bathroom. She took her time in there, and when she came back, she was rewarded by seeing them side-by-side talking animatedly. She walked up behind them quietly, curious to know what exciting topic had drawn them together.

"Those Thornblossoms are terrible!" Fern was saying. "My grandparents just got charged a Questioning Tax because they asked about this dumb statue!"

"Terrible," Osmund agreed. "But only the mayor and the treasurer. If they had a kid, she'd be great, I bet."

Leeva stepped between them. She clasped her hands together behind her back and squeezed them for courage. "They do have a kid, Fern," she said. "Their kid is me." Then she held her breath.

Fern just nodded. "That happens all the time in books. Terrible parents, good kid. Sometimes they're so bad the kid has to run away!"

"Right!" Leeva said in a great rush of pent-up air. "Sometimes they run away! Let's eat cookies!"

After the cookies, they got busy collecting again. The bags were quickly filled.

They scooped up Bob, who actually growled at the early end to his tunneling, and hurried off to Osmund's for three fresh hazmat suits—"waterproof, chemical splash–proof, you'll be glad you have them"—and a quick stop at the library—"Forty-eight orange jelly beans! Goodbye!" Then it was straight to Leeva's house.

Fern did an impressive double take when she saw the library's elevator, and Leeva felt a fresh jolt of horror also. "You're helping me right the wrong," she reminded everyone. Then she quickly reviewed the plan as they got out a huge pot.

Osmund leashed Bob to the refrigerator handle to keep him safe from hot spatters, and then passed out the suits and demonstrated proper wrist and ankle snugging.

Following Fern's instructions, they set a giant pot on the stove, covered the dandelion greens with water, and turned the burner on high.

Soon, the greens began to boil, emitting a strong, but encouraging, scent. Leeva went down to the basement and stacked her arms with newspapers. Back upstairs, she and Osmund dipped the sheets into the pot with tongs, while Fern hung them to dry on the twine they'd strung between the cabinet knobs. The green was just the right shade.

"It's time," Leeva declared. "I'll go upstairs and get the mon—" She gasped and staggered backward. She smacked her hands to her forehead. "Oh, *no!*"

Reader, you remember there had been two problems with her plan. *Two.* In her excitement about solving the first one—dying the paper green—she had completely forgotten the second one.

The really *big* problem.

"What's wrong?" Fern asked.

Leeva pointed up. "The room is locked."

"Where's the key?" Osmund said.

Bob began straining on the leash. "He has a right to be cranky," Leeva explained to Fern. "He needs a certain amount of digging, and we left the park before he'd had it." She crouched down to the badger. "I'm sorry. We'll take you out soon," she promised. She turned to Osmund. "My father wears the key on a chain on his belt. He never lets it out of his sight."

Bob tugged harder, rattling the refrigerator door. He was growing stronger. "Just a minute, Bob," Leeva said. "I have to think."

Reader, if a badger may be said to scowl, this one did. He began scratching at the wall beside the refrigerator. In seconds, his sharp nails shredded the wallpaper and scraped the plaster beneath.

Leeva pulled him back. "He'd go right through that wall if . . . Oh! *OH!*"

And there it was: For the first time in the history of the world, a badger became part of somebody's plan. Fern and Osmund realized it right then, too, because that's how it is with friends.

They brought Bob upstairs. In Leeva's bedroom

closet, they aimed him at the back wall.

Bob looked up at Leeva. *Mine?* his expression asked.

"Yours," Leeva confirmed.

Well, Bob went through the plaster as if it were frosting, and began gnawing with gusto on the wooden laths beneath. In a few moments, he breached the wall and disappeared. Leeva knocked off a few hanging chunks and crawled through after him.

She stood up, surrounded by towers of bulging shoeboxes. She pulled one down and peeled the tape from around its belly. Twenties, fifties, and hundred-dollar bills burst out.

Osmund and Fern crawled in and gaped, but Leeva remained focused. She opened boxes, totaling their amounts, until she felt confident each one contained exactly ten thousand dollars.

"There's plenty of money here to pay all the town institutions their missing three years of budgets," she announced. "But not enough time today. My parents will be back soon and they can't know what we're doing."

She hurried Osmund and Fern out and hid the sheets of dyed newsprint in the cupboards. Then she went to the control panel of the driveway cameras. She had learned many valuable techniques in that detective

novel, including, thank goodness, how to erase security tapes. When she was certain the afternoon's film was gone, she tucked Bob into her backpack and hurried from the house. She plunged through the hedge just as her parents' car cruised in.

Though it was early, it had been a long, exhausting day, so Leeva climbed into the book drop and pulled the quilt around her. She never slept a wink.

LEEVA GETS CLEAN

The next morning, Leeva crouched behind the book drop and watched until she saw her parents leave for work, then crossed the backyard and slipped into her house through the kitchen door.

Up in the money room, she calculated the number of boxes needed to repay the library last year's missing funds, then brought them downstairs. In the kitchen, she took the cash out of the shoeboxes and packed it into Cheap-O Depot grocery bags. Then she refilled the shoeboxes with trimmed green newspaper, taped them up again, and brought them back upstairs and through the hole in her closet.

Leeva was quite fit from exercising with *Vim and Vigor at Any Age*, of course, and her arms had been strengthened by toting ten books a day for weeks, but still, thank goodness for the elevator. Up and down, up and down she rode.

The next order of business was a bath, which, it must be said, Reader, Leeva needed. She dumped in a heaping handful of her mother's celebrity bubble salts and took a nice long soak. All clean and smelling terrific, she dressed in a fresh outfit and fashioned herself a new pair of shoes, doubling the Cheezaroni tray soles—in her new, free life, she was quite a walker and she'd worn clear through her old pair.

Then off to the library. It took five trips, but right before noon, she dropped the last bags on the back stoop.

Harry stepped out. He looked at the bags. "Groceries?"

Leeva shook her head. "Could you please carry your aunt down here? It's important."

Harry looked doubtful, but he went back in.

When he came out with his aunt, Leeva pointed down, too excited to speak.

As Harry and Mrs. Flowers peered into the bags, Leeva could barely keep up with their expressions: astonishment, disbelief, hopefulness, disbelief again, then belief and joy. "Three years of missing library budgets," she told them proudly. Repaying the money made her feel suddenly fresh and clean in a way that had nothing to do with her bath. "My father had it. I've taken it. That's all I'm going to say. I'm going to pay everyone back—"

"Does he know?" Harry broke in. "What happens if he finds out?"

Pauline Flowers shook a finger at her nephew. "She said that's all she's going to say. We don't need to know any more. Finally, new books! Computers!"

Harry still looked worried. "It would be nice to fix the stairs," he admitted.

Leeva hopped from one foot to the other, waiting for the best part to dawn on them.

Mrs. Flowers clasped her hands to her chest. "Story-hour pillows, puppets, tambourines!"

"Health insurance, Aunt Pauline," Harry said.

Leeva couldn't wait one second more. "And *another elevator*!" she broke in.

Mrs. Flowers's eyes brimmed with tears. "I can be a librarian again!"

Leeva turned to Harry. "And you, you can be . . ."

Harry smiled the kind of smile the Clevertons smiled when they were bravely hiding a disappointment.

Leeva guessed he was thinking about the acting school in London. His vanished dream.

She took his hand and gave it a squeeze. "I can't wait to see you in *Our Town* next week. You're going to be wonderful."

"Thanks," Harry said, this time with a real smile.

Although everyone was still extremely excited, Mrs. Flowers insisted they eat. Harry carried the bags of money inside and returned with lunch: stew with chewy bread to dunk and crunchy new apples.

After lunch, Harry brought Leeva the cookies, the thermos, and a new slip of paper.

Leeva found Osmund outside and they gathered up Bob and ran to the address, which was right around the corner. They got the ingredient, dried figs, and left to pick up Fern—no time for chitchat today. They ran back to the library to deliver the figs, and then skidded, panting, into Leeva's kitchen.

There, they set an even larger batch of dandelion leaves on the stove. As it boiled, they shared the cookies—Almond Butter Balls, crunchy with a tart orange jelly bean on top. Then they dipped the newspapers and hung them to dry.

"Today is Thursday. We'll go to the Community

Theater tomorrow," Leeva decided. "Over the weekend, the Parks Department, the Police Station, and the Fire Station. Then the schools on Monday."

"Will I have to talk?" Fern ducked her head.

"No, I'll do it," Leeva assured her. "But even with the three of us, it's too much to carry. Osmund, can you drive your parents' golf cart?"

Osmund fiddled with the Velcro at his cuffs—open, shut, open, shut. Although it was difficult, Leeva kept quiet, letting him decide. Finally Osmund heaved a resigned sigh. "We'll find out tomorrow."

NO ORDINARY GOLF CART

Friday, Leeva ate lunch quickly, ran her errand for Mrs. Flowers in a flash, and was sitting on her own front step by one o'clock. While she waited, she thumbed through the *Nutsmore Weekly*. No actual news, as usual. The word of the week was a good one: *Alacrity—a brisk and cheerful readiness*—although not quite good enough to produce a tingle.

Presently, Osmund pulled into the driveway, and Reader, this was no ordinary golf cart.

It featured shock-absorbing pool noodles duct-taped to the sides and hazard lights looped around the roof. Each seat had a protective harness with a crash helmet. A bugle horn with a black rubber honking-ball was mounted up front to alert pedestrians.

Besides being safe, it was commodious, with padded seats and plenty of room, even once Leeva and Osmund had loaded sixty-one Cheap-O Depot grocery bags stuffed with cash in the back seat and Bob had curled up beside them.

The cart, however, sat motionless in Leeva's driveway.

On the driver's side, Osmund was twisting and grunting. "I'm getting into position. I can't reach the pedals, so I have to drive standing up."

Leeva got out to assess the situation up close, then dashed into her house. A minute later she came out with two blocks of Cheezaroni. "One on each pedal," she explained. "I melted the bottoms so they'll stick. Try it again."

Osmund's feet rested securely now, so off they whizzed.

Driving did not turn out to be difficult. Go. Stop. Steer right, steer left.

Osmund handled the cart neatly down the sidewalk, swerving around blooming dandelions whenever Leeva yelled, *"Watch out!"*

Leeva was tempted to use the word *alacrity*—she'd always wanted to use a word the same day she'd learned it—to describe his driving, but she didn't because while he did display an admirable readiness behind the wheel, it was by no means brisk or cheerful.

Leeva was also tempted to honk that horn, but when she reached for it, Osmund shot her a look that made her shove her hands into her pockets. She took them out often, though, to wave back at the folks who waved at her on street after street. She had not fully realized before just how many people she had met over the summer. "I'm a Thornblossom," she longed to shout to them, "and I'm righting my parents' wrong!" but it was not wise to do that yet.

Soon enough, they picked up Fern, who was waiting on the sidewalk in front of her house, and pulled up in the parking lot behind the Nutsmore Community Theater.

CHEEZARONI TO THE RESCUE

"Bob woke up in a bad mood. I'll stay outside with him," Osmund said.

Leeva slipped Harry's play out of her backpack, where she'd been storing it. She tucked it into the waistband of her shorts to give to someone here for safe-keeping. Then she and Fern walked into the theater.

A woman was sweeping the hall. "Excuse me, please," Leeva said. "We need to speak to whoever is in charge."

The woman tilted her head toward a large door-way. "The director. He's onstage, in the cape. Better not bother him until class is over."

Leeva and Fern followed her nod into a darkened auditorium. Down front, the stage was lit, and on it, a dozen people were flinging themselves about.

"I did it," Fern whispered to Leeva as they waited. "I asked Harry about that acting part. He said it's still open. One of the lines is really important. And he told me his trick for stage fright."

"Did it help?" Leeva whispered back.

"I don't know yet, but I want to try it. He said I need to have one person in the audience, just one person, and pretend he or she is the only person there. Forget everyone else. Direct my acting to that person. It has to be someone I trust. If I did that play next week, would you be my person?"

In the dark, Leeva felt herself glow with pride. "Of course." Of course she would be Fern's person.

Fern crept away to watch the actors up close and Leeva turned her attention to the stage. Harry had told her recently that acting could be subtle or broad. He himself leaned to the Subtle school of acting, and he'd demonstrated by lifting one of his eyebrows a fraction of a hair. "Did you sense it?" he'd asked. "All that intrigue and passion and darkness?" "Yes, all that," Leeva had assured him. "But subtly."

Leeva saw that this director was a Broad type, prone to throat clutching and temple grabbing as he instructed the class.

The students were a mix of styles, but everybody was obviously having a splendid time up on that stage.

Harry should be on that stage, Leeva thought, wishing she had a way to make it happen.

Just as the director swept his hands over his head and called, "Class over!" Osmund came in. "Bob tried to chew through the money bags," he said. "I brought them inside."

He and Leeva marched down to the stage and stood beside Fern. The director spun around.

Leeva was prepared. "Seven hundred thousand, fifty dollars. The money owed to the Community Theater these past three years. You were supposed to get it last year. I'm sorry it was delayed. Don't ask anything more."

The director snorted. But he tossed his cape over one shoulder and strode to the bags.

He peered in. He flung one hand to his forehead and the other skyward. Then he keeled over.

Osmund ran to his side. "I hope he had life insurance."

Leeva knelt by his other side. She held her fingers over his wrist, checking for a pulse. "He's not dead." Then she inspected the man's face carefully.

Reader, a person gets to be quite good at

distinguishing between a heart attack and fainting by watching soap operas, which rely heavily on both for drama. The tip-off is the eyes: squeezed shut, heart attack; fluttered closed, fainted.

"He'll come around with some smelling salts," Leeva announced.

"What are smelling salts?" Fern asked.

"I don't know," Leeva admitted. "I think they're just something that smells . . . loud. Osmund, go pry off one of those Cheezaroni blocks, bring it here, please."

Osmund did, and Leeva waved it under the director's nose.

That did the trick. "Seven hundred thousand, fifty dollars," he marveled, sitting up. "Just in time for the production Thursday night. I have no idea how word spread, but every single person in town has ordered tickets. Well, except for the Thornblossoms, of course. Now we can order folding seats, some speakers for the folks in the back." He got up. "I'd better go."

Leeva nudged Fern. Fern nodded and cleared her throat. "I would like to try out for that young girl's part in your play."

"Can you move your lips?" the director demanded.

Fern stretched her mouth around to show him.

"Better than the mannequin. All right, you're in." He spun away, but Leeva called him back.

"I have something else for you. You know Harry Flowers was writing a play. He was so—"

"Yes, I know. It's a masterpiece," the director interrupted. "Every word a jewel!"

"He was so depressed about having to leave class that he threw it away. But I—"

"Oh, no! Such a shame! It would be a dream to direct it!"

"But I saved it." Leeva pulled out the play. "You keep it, in case he comes back to class."

The director grabbed the pages. "A man can dream!" he cried. "A man *must* dream!" And with a swirl of his cape, he disappeared, pages aloft.

A VERY HARD THING

Fern ran home, eager to tell her family about being in the play.

"Bob really needs to dig, Leeva," Osmund said. "I'll return the golf cart and meet you in the park."

Taking cover behind a parked bus and a series of trees in case her parents should rip the papers from their office windows—*another* of the valuable skills Leeva had learned from that detective book—she walked Bob to the park. There, he took off for the statue pedestal as usual. When Osmund arrived, Leeva saw him scowl at the sign about the upcoming ceremony, but then press his lips shut.

Leeva wished she could thank him for this, but that would mean talking about her parents, which was exactly what she was grateful not to have to do. So instead, she turned the conversation to Bob.

"He's been getting crankier lately. Except when he's outside digging. I've been letting him sleep outside, and he likes that, too, I can tell."

Osmund bit his lip. "He was never happy with me. I don't know why. I made everything perfect for him."

"Maybe perfect isn't . . . perfect," Leeva said gently. "Well, anyway, Bob sure has dug a lot of holes here. There, there, some there . . ." Suddenly, she saw something odd. She pointed to a spot to the right of the pedestal. "Didn't Bob go down over there?"

"Yes." Osmund pointed. "See? That's his tail."

Leeva pointed to a spot on the other side, where a furred snout was poking out. "Then who's that?"

Another badger, this one twice Bob's size, heaved itself out of a hole. Bob sprang out and bounded over to the other badger to give it a nuzzly greeting. The other badger put its paws on Bob's shoulders and began to wash his fur.

"If his parents were killed, this must be another relative," Leeva said. "Maybe an aunt or an uncle. Oh! I think it's like Mrs. Flowers with Harry."

Bob cuddled himself against the bigger badger. He

was making a sound Leeva had never heard him make before. Bob was *purring*.

The purring pleased Leeva, but it also made her throat sting as if a sour lemon were stuck down there. Bob had never cuddled with her. He had never purred under her care. She looked over at Osmund.

He seemed to be having trouble with the same lemon. "Bob's letting us know he's happy," she said cautiously.

Osmund nodded. But he wrapped his arms across his chest. He was trembling. He looked the way Leeva had felt right before she'd asked Harry her urgent, dangerous question a few days ago.

"Would you like a hug, Osmund?" she offered.

Osmund frowned, the way he always did when he was assessing a risk. But after a moment, he turned toward Leeva.

Leeva placed her arms around him and squeezed the same amount that Harry Flowers had. She thought maybe she had done it right, because Osmund stopped trembling. Then she let him go.

It was time to do the thing they both knew had to be done.

"Want me to do it with you?" Leeva offered.

"Yes. I think, yes."

Side by side, Leeva and Osmund walked over to Bob.

"Goodbye," Leeva said. "Have a good life."

Osmund scooped Bob up. He lifted his face shield and dropped a kiss onto Bob's head. His hands shook a little bit as he popped off the collar's safety beads. "Be careful. Watch out for . . . oh, everything." He put the little badger back on the ground. "All right, not everything," he called as Bob waddled off after his aunt or uncle. "But watch out for the big things, okay?"

Osmund was still for a moment, gazing down at the collar. And then he tucked it into his pocket.

"That was really hard," Leeva said as they walked back to the bench. "He was kind of a dud as a pet, but he was *your* dud."

Osmund sat down, not at the very end of the bench as usual, but more in the middle. He stared straight ahead. "*Our* dud."

"Also, he was cranky, but you had to admire how he was *always* cranky. He *persisted* in his crankiness."

"He never slipped. Never once," Osmund agreed.

"I think it is a big risk to love a badger."

"Right. Their fur is so prickly. Almost like a porcupine."

"Well, no, I meant . . . because someday you have to—" Leeva nodded over to where Bob and his aunt or uncle were snuffling around the statue base together.

Osmund's eyes filled.

Which, Leeva noticed, she could see. Osmund hadn't put his face shield back on. Once more, she remembered what a good thing *nothing* was to hear sometimes, and so that's what she said as he unfastened and then refastened the Velcro on his sleeves, his head down.

"It was a good thing, what you just did," she said at last.

Osmund's shoulders lifted slightly.

"I know about a lot of good things you do."

Osmund's suit crinkled as he stiffened, like a warning.

Leeva ignored the warning. "You saved Bob's life. You always defended him. You took risks just being around him, and that must have been hard for you. You worry about people." She pulled the comb from her backpack. "And you gave me *this*."

Osmund raised his head.

Leeva stood up. "I know you and I like you. So would

other people if you didn't scare them away."

Osmund took several sharp breaths in and out through his nose. Finally he straightened up with a decisive shake. He pointed at the comb in Leeva's hand. "Give it to me."

Leeva hesitated. It would hurt to return the first thing she'd ever owned all to herself. But at last she held it out.

Osmund took the comb. He stood up. "Turn around."

Although Leeva suspected Osmund would run away now, she turned around. She held her breath, waiting to hear his boots clomp out of the park. She felt the air still, as if Osmund was holding his breath too, but she didn't hear him leave.

And then she felt him tug the rubber bands from her braids. She felt him unweave her braids and comb out her hair. She felt him divide it into three sections and lay the sections, right-over-center, left-over-center, right-over-center, left-over-center, into a single braid down the middle of her back.

In silence, Osmund and Leeva wobbled their way back to his house, unbalanced by the badger-shaped holes in their lives. The silence was sad, but since it was shared, it was not lonely. And Leeva liked the way the

single braid felt as she walked, giving her a comforting pat between her shoulder blades at every step.

At his doorstep, Leeva thumbed up a backpack strap. "You probably want this back. Now that I don't have Bob."

"Do you have one at home?"

Leeva shook her head.

"Then keep it. You'll need it for school." Then he fished out his keys and started unlocking his door.

Leeva wished that she had something to give Osmund in return. One of the hardest things about not owning anything was that you had nothing to give. But then she realized she did have something. "Wait. May I come in and play SafetyLand?"

Osmund looked back in obvious shock. "Nothing happens in it, you know," he warned.

"I know," she said. "That's perfect."

A HARD TRUTH

Over the weekend, Leeva and Fern and Osmund visited the Parks Department, the Fire Station, and the Police Station. At all three places, they learned a hard truth: Many adults don't believe children simply because they are children. At all three places the adults scoffed when Leeva told them what she was there for, and then keeled over in shock when it turned out to be true, to be revived only by a whiff of Cheezaroni. So at all three places, Reader, the adults learned a hard truth also: Not believing children just because they are children is foolish.

Now, the three children stood in front of the elementary school. Its big front doors were chained, but Leeva liked the look of this place. A rainbow-striped

WELCOME! banner hung over the doorway. A shiny bell looked as if it wanted to ring itself. Swings shifted in a breeze, as if they couldn't wait to get swinging, and a silver slide winked in the morning sun.

This was her school, all right.

Leeva knocked. No answer. She knocked again, harder. Her knocks echoed down vacant hallways, but Leeva was not about to give up. She'd seen cars in the parking lot.

She darted back to the golf cart and honked its horn. (Finally! Worth it! What a sound!)

After a moment, a short, stout woman in a black-and-white dress opened the door. She did not look pleased to have been honked away from whatever she'd been doing.

"That's Principal Heckstrom's secretary," Osmund whispered. "She's like the school's guard dog."

"What are you doing here?" the secretary barked.

"This is our school," Leeva said. "We are expected here next week."

"Yes, that would be correct." The secretary did not seem as impressed as Leeva felt. *"Next week."*

"That includes me," Leeva went on as the full weight of it struck her. "I'll be *right here.*"

The secretary folded her arms across her chest. "But that is *next week*. What are you doing here *now*?"

Leeva drew herself up tall. "The Nutsmore Elementary School is owed three million dollars." She bowed. "I am here to deliver it to Principal Heckstrom."

The secretary snorted at that. "Oh, *reeeeaaallly*? You, a child, are bringing us three million dollars today? And where, I might ask, is it?" She tossed a smirk toward the golf cart. "In those *shopping bags*, perhaps?"

"Actually, yes," Leeva said. "But be prepared. Many people faint when they see it."

The secretary rolled her eyes. But she stomped over to the cart and opened a bag. She clutched her chest, muttering, "Holy moly!" She pointed to the bags. "There's money in there!"

Leeva was relieved this woman was not a teacher. You'd have to worry about this person teaching anyone anything. "Yes," she confirmed. "That's what I said."

The secretary spluttered another "Holy moly!" With that, she keeled over, stiff as a drunken penguin, feet up.

"Here we go again." Osmund pulled off a Cheezaroni block and, once more, this did the trick.

The woman got to her feet. "I'll get Principal Heckstrom," she mumbled meekly, backing into the building.

Principal Heckstrom, a young woman wearing a snappy red tracksuit, emerged and strode over. "Hello, Osmund, hello, Fern," she greeted them. She turned to Leeva. "Three million dollars? Our missing funds?" she asked crisply.

Leeva liked her right away. This woman didn't mess around. "Correct."

"Excellent news." Principal Heckstrom hefted two of the bags with an ease that suggested both vim and vigor. "Let's get these inside. Got to order supplies. School starts next week."

"I know! I'm coming!" Leeva couldn't help blurting out.

"Even better news," Principal Heckstrom said, and Leeva could tell she meant it. "We could use a new student with your obvious academic alacrity."

WHAT DAY IS THIS?

L ater that morning, as they loaded the cart for the final two deliveries, Leeva said, "There's still a lot of money upstairs."

"It belongs to the townspeople," Osmund said. "It was stolen from them. All those fake taxes."

Leeva, recalling the town report, made a quick calculation. "Nutsmore's population is six hundred ten people. There's enough to give each person eight thousand, four hundred sixty dollars."

"Our neighbor had twins last week," Fern reported.

Leeva began to recalculate, but then she thought of something. "My parents are the ones who stole the money. They don't get any. Eight thousand, four hundred sixty dollars each. The problem is, even with the golf cart, it will take forever to make so many deliveries."

"Too bad they can't all come to the same place at the same time," Fern said.

"That's it!" Leeva cried. "Everyone is coming to the play Thursday night. Everyone except my parents. So it's perfect."

"Everyone?" Fern blanched, hand to her throat. "That's a lot of people! Make sure you sit up front, where I can see you."

"We'd better dye another batch of newspapers," Osmund said. "A big one."

They went back inside and suited up. When the kitchen was once again hung with wet green newsprint, they buckled themselves into the golf cart and rolled off.

At the middle school, the familiar scenario played out: Leeva told the adult in charge what she was going to do, the adult in charge scoffed in disbelief, Leeva did what she'd said she was going to do, and then the adult keeled over in shock that she'd actually done it. Some adults, really!

The final stop was the high school, which was quite a ways out, as if Nutsmore had decided that teenagers, like gangsters and infectious diseases, should be penned up at a safe distance.

Osmund shared this view of them. "The risk of crashes is higher for people sixteen through nineteen than any other age group," he said as they drove. "In fact, they get into so much trouble they shouldn't be allowed out at all."

"Not all of them," Leeva argued. "Harry Flowers is a teenager."

"Harry's different," Osmund allowed.

"And it's a good thing he wasn't locked away," Leeva went on. "Everywhere you go, someone has a story about some nice thing he did." She turned to look at Osmund. She'd never heard why he liked Harry so much.

Osmund took his eyes off the road long enough to glance over at Leeva, then Fern. "Me, too. Harry did something really nice for me once." He took a breath so deep his suit rustled. "He gave me my first hazmat suit."

"Harry did?" Leeva asked. "Why?"

"I used to be really nervous," Osmund said. "A couple of years ago. I couldn't even leave my house. It was terrible. Mrs. Flowers sent him over with some books, and he asked me to tell him about it. The next day, he brought me a suit. He said it would protect me so I could stop worrying about things. He said I wouldn't need it forever, but while I did I should wear it, no matter what anyone said about it. He was right. I could go out after that."

"Harry's the best," Fern said.

Osmund nodded. "Always. Except . . ."

"Except what?" Leeva asked.

"Well, about a month ago, he said he had sent me something. The way he talked, I thought it was going to be something great."

"And wasn't it?"

"I don't know. I checked the mail every day, and nothing came. I guess he forgot."

Fern spoke up. "Me, too. The exact same thing, a few weeks ago. He said to keep watch for something wonderful coming. I never saw it."

This didn't seem like Harry, Leeva thought, but that wasn't the point. "Well, everyone is a teenager sometime."

Osmund shook his head. "I'll be that age, but I won't *be* one."

And Leeva realized he was kind of right. Osmund was already like an adult—a miniature adult in a hazmat suit. "Maybe not," she said. "But remember what I said the other day, that what you get from your parents is like a . . . like a golf cart?"

Osmund patted the dashboard. "They didn't actually give it to me."

"Right, but I meant . . . you could drive it any way you want. And you could go anywhere you choose."

"Well, within a twenty-mile range. Then it needs a charge."

"No, I meant . . . you could fill your car with friends, or—"

"Or bags of money," Osmund said, glancing back.

Leeva gave up then. They had arrived at the high school.

"My sister goes here," Fern said. "Principal Buggums is always in a bad mood. I'll wait in the cart."

Principal Buggums himself answered their knock, frowning. Leeva knew it was him because he wore a large lapel pin that read *Principal Buggums*. Also because he was flanked by two men wearing lapel pins that read *Principal Buggums's Staff*.

"I am Principal Buggums," he said, as if the pins weren't enough. "What do you want? I'm very busy. I've lots to do."

It occurred to Leeva that such a busy person probably shouldn't waste time repeating himself, but now wasn't the time to point that out. She launched into the announcement she had prepared. "We have brought you something. It is a good something, Principal Buggums, but it is shocking."

"Are you insured against fainting?" Osmund asked.

"I am not," Principal Buggums answered. "I am uninsured."

"I've brought a policy." Osmund patted his pocket.

"That won't be necessary. I don't need it. What is this something? What have you brought me?"

"Not yet." Leeva couldn't help noticing that Principal Buggums did not have a single hair on his head. If he went over, his skull would crack like an egg.

She ran back to the golf cart for a seat pad. She judged the principal's height, then positioned the pad on the concrete where his head would land. "Insurance," she told him. "To cushion the blow against possible loss of consciousness." Then she delivered the news. "We have brought you three million dollars, the amount owed to you from last three years."

Reader, once more: scoffing, peering into bags, keeling over, *thunk!*

The principal's head landed smack on the cushion and did not crack. He got up and turned to his staff. "Gather these bags, pick them up. Take them inside, into the school," he ordered. He turned to Leeva. "I've got to get going, lots to do. School starts in one week." He checked a notebook. "Yes, seven days, exactly. Next Monday. Last Monday of the month."

Leeva said goodbye quickly and headed for the parking lot with Fern and Osmund. They had done their job here, and done it well, but Fern had been right about Principal Buggums and his crabby mood. As they hopped into the golf cart, though, something struck Leeva. Something terrible.

"Did he say . . . Is this the third Monday of the month?"

"It is," Fern said. "Why?"

Leeva grabbed Osmund's suit so hard the sleeve tore. "Drive!" she yelled. "As fast as you can!"

NOPE!

Her parents' car was in the driveway, engine still ticking. "You two get out of here," Leeva ordered Osmund and Fern as she jumped out of the golf cart.

She tore around to the back door. If she could only get into the kitchen in time . . .

Too late.

Before she could hide a single incriminating sheet of newspaper, her father stumbled in, red-faced and sweating, with a month's worth of Cheezaroni. He dumped the Cheap-O Depot grocery bags on the floor and then collapsed over the counter.

And then, as he caught his breath, he looked around.

Swamped with dread, Leeva saw him take in the

daughter who'd run away and the kitchen hung with green newspapers.

He straightened up. His jaw fell open. He nodded with a crafty smile. "Yes, good," he crooned. "I won."

Leeva had been worried about a range of responses, from bad to horrible. This was not one of them. "You won?"

Still nodding and smiling at the green newspapers, her father pulled out a Cheezaroni block and unwrapped it. He gnawed off a corner and munched. "I've been arguing with your mother all week that we're not paying for a drape for that statue unveiling when you could make one out of newspapers. Obviously, I won." He stuffed another orange hunk into his mouth and closed his eyes as he chomped.

Leeva was astonished. Somehow, her father hadn't registered the fact that she'd run away! Somehow, she was safe.

But then he opened his eyes, frowning.

Leeva held her breath, her heart pounding so hard she was sure he would hear it.

He cocked his head at the newsprint. "There's something about the green. What is it?" he mumbled. "I don't know why, but I like it." He kicked the bags. "Cook these up. We're going back to work."

"Yes, better hurry," Leeva encouraged him, motioning toward the door. But then she realized what he had just said. "We?" she asked. "Who is 'we'?"

"Your mother's upstairs. She came back with me to change her shoes, said they weren't sharp enough."

Her father wandered out and Leeva closed the door after him. She quickly unpinned the papers. It had been a narrow escape, but it was over, she told her racing heart. Her mother never came into the kitchen.

But while Leeva was stacking the papers, the door burst open. In stepped her mother, *clink-clink-clink.* "Your father said you're making a drape for my—" She stopped in the center of the kitchen. She gaped at the appliances. She spread her hands in flummoxed bewilderment.

"Stove," Leeva supplied. "Refrigerator. This is a kitchen."

Leeva's mother nodded doubtfully. She caught her reflection in a hanging pan, and this seemed to reassure her. She blew a kiss at her reflection, then waved at the stack of dyed newspapers. "Get rid of them. I wouldn't drape a golden statue in newspapers."

"The whole thing is golden now?" Leeva asked,

surprised. "Not just the shoes?"

"All of it. Gold-plated, head to toe. I fired that numbskull sculptor last week, found another. And just in time. The ceremony is Thursday night."

"Thursday night? But that's the night of the play."

"Exactly. The whole town will be there. And it's not an unveiling anymore—that wasn't going to be a powerful enough statement. I'm having the statue delivered by helicopter now."

Leeva doubted the people of Nutsmore would stick around after the play to see a statue of her mother even if it was flown in by helicopter, but she was wise enough not to say this. Besides, something odd was happening to her mother's face. Was she *smiling*?

"Which was it?" Mayor Thornblossom asked. She was definitely smiling.

"What?"

"You've been gone. You're only allowed to leave to get us more money or fame. So, which was it?" Her smile widened. "Am I more famous?"

Leeva's father poked his head into the doorway, licking his fingers. "Or am I richer?"

Leeva was flabbergasted. *This* was what they'd been worried about all week? "Neither. I didn't do either."

Her father's face folded in disappointment. Her mother's face lost the smile. "Then where have you been?" she asked.

Leeva considered carefully. She had done what she'd set out to do: given back the stolen money to all Nutsmore's institutions. In a few days, the rest of it would be returned to the people. She had righted the wrong and she was a criminal no longer. Whatever punishment her parents could dish out, well, she could take it.

"I have been with people, all over town," she said, feeling the great relief of telling a truth you are proud of. "I've been to the library. I've been to all the schools and the Community Theater, too. And the Police Station and the Fire Station and the Parks Department."

"Those are all town buildings," her mother noted mildly. She checked herself in the hanging pan again, pooched her lips, *smuck*, *smuck*. "You saw my portrait everywhere you went?"

Leeva threw her hands up in disbelief. "Actually, no. None of those places have your portrait up. While I was gone, did you ever wonder if I was all right?"

Mayor Thornblossom narrowed her eyes. "None of those places?" *Scritch-scritch*. "Well, I guess I'll have to close them all down."

"What? No!" Leeva gasped. "You can't do that!"

Her mother leaned in. "I'm the mayor."

The thing in Leeva's chest that hated unfairness, her righteous indignation, stirred. "But you're supposed to punish *me* for leaving, remember? Not . . ." She was overwhelmed for a moment trying to calculate who would be hurt by this threat. "Not *everyone*. Not *the whole town*."

Mayor Thornblossom shrugged.

At the heartless shrug, the righteous indignation crouched low and began to growl. *No, stay down*, she willed it. *It's not a good time.*

It didn't listen. It began to circle as if it was centering itself. Gathering strength. It had waited a lifetime and it was *done waiting*.

Really. Please, Leeva tried again. *It's too dangerous.*

Her mother shrugged again. "I'll close them all. I can and I will."

And the righteous indignation sprang up, both fists raised hard, and it bellowed, through Leeva's lips, a single powerful word . . .

"NOPE!!!"

The word had a lot of oomph. Plenty of pizzazz. It exploded through the startled kitchen. Pots rattled

and spoons shook. Leeva and her parents stared at each other, six eyes popped like ping-pong balls.

"Nope?" her father repeated as if he'd never heard the word.

"Nope!"

"Nope?" Mayor Thornblossom asked, tapping her ears as if she couldn't believe what she'd heard.

The thing in Leeva's chest expanded, full and strong. "Nope. I'll take my punishment for leaving. And I won't do it again. But you will *leave them open*."

Her mother hoisted both eyebrows. "No more of this *I-want-to-be-with-people* nonsense? You won't go anywhere?"

Leeva held her head high. She knew better than to ask about the exceptions—she'd never be able to bring her parents more fame or money. Tears stung, but she squeezed them back. "No more. I won't go anywhere. But you must leave them all open."

"Ha! We won," her mother said.

"Now stop talking and go away," her father added.

And Leeva did.

THE CENTER OF EVERYTHING

Only a few weeks ago, Leeva had had no knowledge of libraries or librarians, badgers or book drops, hugs or cookies or kittens or toast. But now, after enjoying these riches for only a few weeks, it was torture to lose them.

For two days she tried to return to her old ways. She slogged from room to room picking things up, dusting and wiping, but now it nearly numbed her into a coma. She duly scissored herself into the air for the opening jumping jacks on *Vim and Vigor at Any Age*, but when the trainers cried, *"You can do it, you are vimful and vigorous!"* she sobbed back, *"No, I can't, Jim! No, I'm not, Jilly!"* and then snapped off the television.

At noon, she rolled a sturdy newspaper tube,

shellacked it with her mother's all-weather hairspray, and carried it to the backyard. She worked it through the hedge until she had a clear view. "I'm here, and you're here," she would call to Harry when she saw him come out to the stoop. "We can still talk."

But Harry didn't come out.

Leeva went back inside and cut a wedge of Cheeza-roni, but with the first bite the orange sludge clogged her throat shut.

She turned the television back on for *The Winds of Our Tides*, but while it was exciting—the evil impostors were now trying to fool the Clevertons' own daughters!—it only reminded her of the real people she was no longer with.

And she tried to write to the Flowerses. *Thank you for trusting me. If you don't mind, I will keep my library card. I will miss you more than there are words.* But each time, she tore the letter in half. It was too painful to write the word *goodbye* to Harry and Pauline Flowers.

Now, as the second afternoon wound to a close, Leeva stood at her bedroom window looking at the library.

Technically, she could still *see* the Flowerses, she reminded herself—if the light struck a window just right and one of them happened to be passing by. She pressed her forehead to the glass and watched, but neither of them appeared.

Anyway, seeing them wouldn't be enough. It surprised Leeva how much she wanted *them* to see *her*. Whenever Harry or his aunt had looked at her, she had known that she *mattered*.

A movement at the second-floor window caught her attention. She saw a girl pull a book off a shelf. How lucky that girl was, choosing books, being able to curl up in a commodious armchair or talk to Harry, with the scent of Mrs. Flowers's cookies drifting through the air.

But . . . what if Mrs. Flowers asked that girl if she'd like some of those cookies? What if Harry invited her to have lunch out on the back stoop with him?

Leeva yanked her curtains shut so hard the newspaper tore. She flung herself on her bed. The Flowerses would find other kids to care about. They would forget all about her.

Oh, life, she thought. If her parents hadn't asked her *What are people for?*, she'd never have gone into the library, trying to find out. If she'd never gone into the library, she'd never have met Harry and Mrs. Flowers. In fact, if her parents hadn't stolen the library's money,

Harry wouldn't be here at all, and he'd never have sent her for ingredients and she'd never have met Osmund and Bob and Fern and all the others, and she wouldn't be missing all of them so much now.

Life! Life rolled on, simple and complicated, funny and not, terrible and wonderful. She felt she was just getting the hang of it, and now look, she was locked away again!

Leeva's thoughts were spiraling away tragically like this when she heard a knock at the door. She dragged herself out of bed.

There, on her front step, was Osmund. "I was worried," he said.

Leeva explained that she couldn't come out anymore. Then she arranged for him to stop by the next day to pick up the money packets and hand them out at the play. "At least I can finish righting that wrong," she said, waving goodbye.

Osmund didn't move. "I was *worried*," he said again. "Fern, too. You should have let us know."

"Oh." Never before had Leeva had to let anyone know what was happening to her. Never before had anyone cared. "Thank you, Osmund," she said. "I'm sorry."

Osmund left and Leeva dialed Fern. Before she

could tell her what had happened, Fern asked a favor: "Could you listen while I practice my part?"

Leeva said, "Sure," and carried the phone to her thinking spot and slid down onto the floor.

Harry was right that Fern's part was small, only a few lines. And it turned out that her big one—the one Harry said was so important—was only an address.

"Okay, imagine me holding an envelope," Fern said. And then she read an address that went on and on. After the street and town, it continued into country, continent, planet, solar system—all the way up to universe. Fern packed a lot of emotion into it. Halfway in, Leeva was feeling chills. Still.

"What makes that line so important?" Leeva asked.

"Harry says it means that wherever you are, you can imagine it as the center of everything. Even if it's a little place like . . . oh, like the Nutsmore Park, it's the center of the universe because what happens to people there happens to people everywhere. It's universal."

Fern practiced her part again, and then she shuddered so dramatically Leeva could feel her worry over the phone. "Sit close to the stage so I can find you tomorrow night, okay?"

Leeva sat bolt upright. She had offered to be Fern's

person in the audience tomorrow night! The one Fern could trust.

"I'll be there at eight o'clock," she promised. "Right up front."

Sitting there in her thinking spot, Leeva felt a cold dread gather in her belly. What had she just done? If she were caught leaving the property again, there was no telling what her punishment might be. Worse, her mother would close every place down and punish the entire town of Nutsmore.

Her parents absolutely, positively could not see her tomorrow night.

A BIRTHDAY

Thursday morning, Leeva woke up a nervous wreck. But she was also excited. If she had only a few hours of freedom, there was nowhere she'd rather spend them than at the play, where she could be with everyone she cared about one final time.

At breakfast, her parents were chipper, too. "I'll be so famous!" her mother crowed, between glugs of coffee. "Admission, ten dollars!" her father gloated over his Cheezaroni.

Leeva's mood only improved through the day. When Jim and Jilly assured her she was vimful and vigorous, she could do it, she shouted back, "Oh, yes, I *am*, Jim! Oh, yes, I *can*, Jilly!" During *The Winds of Our Tides*, the Cleverton daughters exposed the evil impostors in a dramatic courtroom scene. When they threw their arms to point out who they really belonged with and the judge rapped his gavel in their favor, the courtroom went bananas and Leeva went bananas with them.

When Osmund came for the packets, she told him the news. "It's only for one night, but it will be the best of my life."

"What if you get caught?"

"It'll be bad," Leeva admitted. "But it will be worth it. Will you braid my hair again?"

After Osmund left, Leeva put her newest dress on inside out, so it was less worn, and styled a pillowcase around her shoulders the way Pauline Flowers wore her scarves. Lastly, she wove herself a pair of strappy red-and-yellow sandals from a glossy pizza brochure that had been stuck in her door. She didn't put the shoes on yet, though, fearing her parents might comment on her appearance when she served them dinner.

As it turned out, neither one noticed.

When Leeva set down her mother's plate, the fork rattled slightly. "Quiet!" Her mother shot her a warning glare, then turned back to her show. "Famous in a flash," she muttered. "It should be me. One day it will be me . . ."

Mr. Thornblossom didn't even look at her when she set his plate down. He was pretending to be fully engrossed in an ad. Leeva knew he was pretending because the ad was for a flyswatter and anyone could see how easy it would be to fashion one for free out of newspaper.

Leeva waited silently on her stool, musing that sometimes it is a blessing to be ignored. She collected the dishes and once again neither parent said anything about how she looked. But just as she left the room, her father yelled, "Leeva!"

Leeva tensed in the doorway. *Please, please, please don't ask why I'm dressed up*, she begged. "Yes, Father?"

"Go make me a flyswatter."

Leeva dropped off the dishes and whooshed down to the basement. There, she expertly fashioned a newspaper flyswatter: rolled tube for a handle and folded pages for a slapper pad, punched through with aerodynamic holes. She taped the pieces together, rode the elevator back upstairs, and laid the flyswatter by her father's side.

Her father shook an I-told-you-so finger at her.

"Ha! Old newspapers, that's the solution," he crowed.

Well, Reader, Leeva certainly agreed with that.

The instant they drove away, Leeva stepped outside. The air that evening sparkled crisp as ginger ale. Leeva drank it in, fizzy with excitement.

Sticking to the shadows, she made her way to the park. It looked different tonight. Strings of lights lit the paths, glinting off shiny new playground equipment and just-painted benches. A fresh scent blew off the new-mown lawns.

Leeva realized that she was responsible for the trimmed grass and the other improvements in the park, and she wished she could go enjoy them. But her parents were in that park—she'd overheard them planning to set up loudspeakers and searchlights. She snuck around the back way to the theater.

Osmund was already there, with the packets of money beside the two large front doors. He looked different tonight, too, and it took Leeva a moment to realize what it was. "You look really nice," she said. "No hazmat suit."

"I don't need it anymore," he explained, looking almost as surprised as Leeva felt. "And besides, it's not

me I'm worried about tonight." He gestured to the packets at his feet. "We have to make everyone promise not to open them until they're home, sitting down. We can't revive hundreds of people before the show even starts."

This was obviously a wise plan, and so it was exactly what they did. After they saved good seats in the front row, each of them took a door. "Enjoy the show; don't open this until you are sitting down at home," they were soon greeting everyone.

Shortly, Leeva saw Harry and his aunt in the crowd. She waved them to her door. Both of them hugged her, and Leeva tried to imprint their hugs on her body, so she could remember them forever. Then she gave them their packets with the strict warning, wished Harry luck as he hurried backstage, and told Mrs. Flowers where she'd saved her a seat.

Fern and her big family came through—fifteen packets went in with them. Fern turned back as they left and called out, "Don't forget to wave so I can find you, Leeva."

The woman next in line gasped. "Leeva? Leeva *Spayce*? Is it you?"

Leeva gasped, too, as she realized who the woman must be. "Nurse Blackberry?"

The woman clasped her chest. "I held you the first hour of your life. And now look at you!"

"Oh! Do you know when that was? Do you know my birthday?"

"Why, exactly! March fourth. I remember because I said to myself, this little girl has got something special, and boy, is she going to need it. She's going to need to march forth, all right. It's good to see you doing so well. I lost track of you once you weren't in the paper all the time."

"I was in the paper?"

"Every day, for your first month. Your mother insisted she be photographed holding you."

"She *held* me?" Leeva tried to picture this, but it required more imagination than she had.

"Well, she didn't exactly *hold* you. You were usually slung over her shoulder. Like . . ." Nurse Blackberry paused in thought. The thought seemed to infuriate her. "Unbelievable. She held you like a *pocketbook*." Nurse Blackberry muttered, "Like a *pocketbook*!" again as she took her packet and went in, shaking her head.

For another ten minutes, excited townspeople, including reporters from the *Nutsmore Weekly* and Station K-NUTZ television, poured into the theater. When the last person was inside, there were still two packets left.

"Did we count wrong?" Osmund asked.

"No, I'm certain not," Leeva said. Then it hit her. "They're *ours*! You and I—*we* are Nutsmorians, too!" They closed the front doors, and went inside just as the lights dimmed. Osmund found his parents and Leeva took her seat beside Mrs. Flowers. A pianist began to play softly and the stage curtains parted, revealing the actors on a spare set with only a few scenery props—a tree, a desk, and a chair.

Leeva raised her hand toward Fern and crossed her fingers in the secret symbol of good luck. Fern smiled and swept a deep bow in her direction.

Suddenly, the loudspeakers outside screeched to life.

"AS OF THIS EVENING," a voice shrieked into the theater, "IT IS ILLEGAL TO PERFORM *OUR TOWN*!!! THE OFFENSE IS PUNISHABLE BY

JAIL TIME AND ENORMOUS FINES!!! EXIT THE BUILDING THROUGH THE FRONT DOORS NOW!!!"

Leeva knew that voice all too well.

And Reader, she had *had* it with that voice.

TRAPPED!

Leeva Thornblossom marched forth, right onto the stage, where the actors were milling around in shock and the director was tearing at his hair in a dramatic fashion. She tugged on Harry's sleeve. "These people came to see a play. My mother didn't forbid yours."

"But I destroyed mine," Harry said. "You saw."

"No, Harry. I saved it." She caught the director's eye. Acting broadly, she mimed getting Harry's pages. A minute later, the director was handing out copies to the actors.

While they huddled with Harry, Leeva took the microphone. She addressed the audience in a clear, sure voice. "Harry Flowers told me you can see what's most important in what ordinary people do. Like Harry. He's an ordinary person. But all of you that I've met this summer have told me about something special he did. Harry's written a play. Let's watch Harry's play."

The audience answered with uncertain applause, and the actors took their places.

The director stepped to the center of the stage and cleared his throat. "*The Question*, by Harold Flowers," he announced.

Leeva snuggled down into her seat. Harry's play was bound to be a good one.

Onstage, Harry, playing a teenager named Paul Weeds, was slumped over a desk. A woman in a purple wig—Harriet Weeds—stood beside him, rubbing her knees.

Fern walked up to them. "Hello, my name is Theeva Lornblossom," she read to Harry's character. "I want to know: What are people for?"

Leeva snapped upright. Theeva Lornblossom? Harriet and Paul Weeds? Hmm . . .

Onstage, as the Weedses reflected on the question Theeva had asked, they came to see that they were both lonely: The Paul character was lonely for his actor-self and for all the different paths he wasn't walking. His aunt was lonely for her librarian-self and all the people she missed choosing books for.

The audience sighed in empathy. And it struck Leeva then that the world was full of loneliness. Osmund was lonely for people he was afraid to allow near. Fern was lonely for the family she missed. Leeva, herself, had been utterly lonely her whole life, until this summer.

The audience sighed again, this time in relief, as the characters came to understand it all. But then came an upsetting scene: When Paul Weeds gave up *his* dream in order to purchase an elevator so his aunt could have *her* dream, his aunt grew extremely upset. "Theeva was right when she said that people are for sharing life. So how could I be happy when you've made yourself so unhappy?"

"That's exactly what Theeva said," the Paul character said next. "She's a real treasure."

"We love her," the aunt character agreed. "We truly do."

As those last lines were read, Leeva began to shine.

Reader, when you know you are loved—whether the knowledge comes as a surprise like this, or whether you are lucky enough to have grown up with it—you actually *shine*. The shine is love reflected. It is a soft and healing light, like the moon's glow over a dark and aching world.

When Mrs. Flowers reached over and squeezed Leeva's hand, Leeva was sure that her luminescence must be bathing the entire theater.

The actors took their bows and the folks of Nutsmore just went wild. They stomped their feet and clapped, waving anything that could be waved.

Leeva was glad Fern's great-grandparents had trained with *Vim and Vigor at Any Age*, because they would surely have injured themselves otherwise, leaping about so enthusiastically. Osmund and his parents threw their cautious natures out the window, applauding with dangerous abandon. Mrs. Flowers wept tears of joyful pride.

Harry had written a smash.

"Bravo, bravo, bravo!" the cries went on. Only after a dozen curtain calls did the audience finally begin to leave.

Just as Leeva had expected, everyone headed for the back door to avoid the statue ceremony. But right away, a murmur of protest arose. The murmur grew to a rumble as the bad news spread—the back door was barred from the outside!

The fire chief stood on the police chief's shoulders and ordered everyone to turn around and exit calmly through the two front doors.

There, though, was more bad news: Fencing, which must have been put in place during the show, would funnel everyone across the street and into the park.

Leeva wormed her way up to the front so she could see. The fencing widened into a ring, lit by spotlights, around the statue pedestal. Her mother preened on tall scaffolding beside it and her father clutched a shoebox.

The people of Nutsmore were trapped into attending that statue ceremony and paying for it, too.

And Leeva's parents were absolutely, positively going to see her.

THE AMAZING IDEA

Leeva dashed back inside and onto the stage. She slipped her packet of money into the pillowcase around her neck to free her hands, then grabbed the scenery tree's trunk. Carrying it in front of her, she made her way out of the theater and right up to the crowd at the statue pedestal. She edged between Harry and his aunt.

Harry patted a branch with a chuckle. Mrs. Flowers winked through the silk leaves. And Leeva felt safer, even when her father passed by only inches away, collecting ten dollars admission from everyone.

Evening had fallen, deep and cool. Leeva felt comfortable outside at night now, and the constellations felt like friends. She was just tracing Pegasus when she noticed a dot of light at the horizon that seemed to be moving.

A bank of searchlights snapped on, targeting that moving dot of light. Six hundred twelve people looked up.

As it grew closer, the dot revealed itself to be a helicopter, whirring and thumping across the night sky. Swinging from its landing skids was an enormous golden statue.

The helicopter hovered over the park and began its descent, its blades churning the trees' canopy. Startled Nutsmorians scooped up toddlers and clutched hats. The branches of Leeva's tree whipped back and forth.

The crowd shrank back as those colossal stilettos loomed over them like daggers. The newspaper reporter and the television newscaster aimed their cameras.

Down, down, down came the statue. Just when it was positioned over its base, Leeva remembered something: as a cost-saving measure, her father had ordered the pedestal designed to withstand *only* the weight of the statue *with gold-plated shoes.* But now the *entire thing* was gold-plated, and gold, she knew from memorizing the periodic table of elements, was one of the heaviest elements on earth.

"*STOP!*" she screamed. "*Don't unhook the chains! The*

pedestal won't hold!"

No one heard, of course, amid the deafening *whomp-whomp-whomp* of the helicopter rotors.

The helicopter released the chains and whirred off.

The statue crashed onto the pedestal.

And then, with a deep rumbling, it kept going.

And *going*.

"Bob's been digging there!" Osmund yelled, waving away clouds of rubble. "The tunnels are collapsing! Stay back! It's an uninsurable risk!"

Everyone heeded Osmund's order. Except for the one person on the scene who could not abide being told what to do.

Up on the scaffolding, Mayor Thornblossom howled like a wounded hyena, then dove headfirst into the pit after her likeness. Down, she hurtled, down, down into the bowels of the park. Into her own crypt.

The crowd gasped and surged forward.

Swiftly, Mr. Thornblossom was there with his shoebox out. "Another ten dollars to view the disaster!"

At the edge of the pit, the reporter from the *Nutsmore Weekly* scratched madly in her notebook. The station K-NUTZ newscaster aimed his video camera into the pit and held up a microphone. "The mayor is moving,"

he announced. "Looks like she's all right. But she seems
to be hung up on those giant stilettos . . ."

"Robbie Flamble!" Mrs. Flowers called out. "Lefty
Sluggins! Little Mario Junior! Where are you?"

Three men pushed through the crowd. Quickly, fire-
men hooked ropes to their belts and lowered the men
into the hole.

"A daring rescue has begun," the K-NUTZ newscaster reported. His microphone picked up a torrent
of words from the pit, which would have to be bleeped
out.

Leeva edged her tree away—she knew the sounds of her mother's fury.

"Show's over! Stop talking and go away!" Mayor Thornblossom ordered everyone when she was finally hauled out.

The crowd began to rush from the park, but Harry and Pauline hid with Leeva behind her tree. They watched the mayor lunge at the reporters, wielding the giant crystals from the statue's shoes.

The *Nutsmore Weekly* reporter took a final picture, then hurried off with the end of the crowd.

As the K-NUTZ newscaster packed up his video camera in obvious terror, Leeva had an idea.

An amazing, brilliant, crazy idea.

She made her way over to the newscaster and whispered instructions in his ear, "Tell them what happened here, and send them the film."

The newscaster dialed a number. Leeva listened intently as he explained the situation, to make sure he told it all. "Yes, that's right, a statue of herself . . . terrible crash . . . death-defying jump . . . yes, swan dive, right in, after the statue of herself . . . I'm sending the film now." He hung up and pressed some buttons on his camera. After only a minute, his phone rang.

The newscaster's eyes ballooned. "Ma'am. S'cuse me. Mayor Thornblossom," he said, holding the phone out with a trembling hand. "It's for you."

Mayor Thornblossom snatched the phone.

As the newscaster's microphone was still on, Leeva and the Flowerses heard the exchange. "We watched the footage! Risking your life for a statue of yourself—that's the stuff! Congratulations, you're . . . *Famous in a Flash!*"

"Finally! I'll leave tonight!" Mayor Thornblossom shrieked into the phone. She turned to Leeva's father. "Are you coming with me?"

Reader, you know what Leeva's father asked: "Will it bring us more money?"

Well, the answer was *Quite a lot*, so his answer was *Yes*.

"We'll leave now!" Leeva's mother shouted.

"Not yet!" her father yelled. "We have to stop at home first. Our treasure is there—"

"You're right!" Leeva's mother screamed. "So precious, so valuable!" Leeva's parents tore off toward the parking lot.

Mrs. Flowers pushed aside some branches to look at Leeva. "They're going back to get you."

Leeva was surprised to see that Pauline Flowers was

crying. She dropped the tree. "What's wrong?"

Mrs. Flowers dabbed her eyes with her scarf. "Nothing, nothing. You must hurry. Your parents are going home for you, and you must be there."

Leeva was torn. She had just been called a treasure, precious and valuable, by her parents. It felt deliciously satisfying.

But she had also just learned that Harry and Pauline called her a treasure, too. She'd learned that they loved her.

"Come on, Leeva," Harry said, taking her hand. "We'll drive you."

Harry tore along the back roads and skidded into the library parking lot.

Leeva jumped out. She tried to say goodbye to Harry and his aunt, but the word was still impossible. "Please don't forget me!" she cried instead, then she bolted to the hedge and broke through.

PRECIOUS TREASURE

L eeva stood alone in her dark kitchen, waiting.

In a few moments, she heard the front door open and the elevator whoosh upstairs. From above came a muffled thumping.

Leeva went into the hall. The elevator began its descent. The door slid open. Her parents staggered out, her father loaded with shoeboxes, her mother wielding her full-length mirror.

"I'm here," Leeva said. "Your treasure."

Her parents bumped past her and out the front door. They didn't seem to notice her as they hurried in and out, whooshed up and down, carting boxes and boxes of worthless green paper, and more and more mirrors, out to the car.

Leeva followed them outside after their last load. Standing in front of the car, she lifted her chin. "Here I am."

Through the windshield, she saw her father buckle a seat belt over the shoebox pressed to his chest. She saw her mother check her image in the mirror, then stick the key into the ignition.

Of course, Leeva told herself, her parents didn't know! They didn't know that she was responsible for getting the news to "Famous in a Flash." They didn't know that finally, she had brought them more money and more fame.

They didn't know that finally, she was the daughter they'd always wanted.

Surely, if she told them, they would not drive away without her. She planted her hands on the hood of the car.

Just then, her mother flipped on the headlights. Leeva was momentarily blinded by their harsh glare, the exact opposite of the soft and healing glow of reflected love.

Her parents rolled down their windows and stuck out their heads. "We're off to be famous! Famous in a flash!" her mother called. "And rich!" her father said.

"See you in ten years!"

It was now or never. Leeva opened her mouth. But what she said was not, "I brought you this money and fame."

What she said was, "Stop talking and go away."

And Leeva's parents did.

They hadn't heard her over the eager revving of the engine. Yet they stopped talking and turned the car around and went away.

Leeva stood there, watching, until their taillights disappeared.

She stood there a long time after that.

She stood there until she realized that she was extremely tired. She was as tired as if she'd been trying to push an enormous boulder her whole life and had finally given up.

She should go to bed. She turned to her house. No, not in there. Where she wanted to be was in the book drop, with its soft quilt and Harry and Pauline Flowers nearby.

With her last bit of energy, she dragged herself around to the backyard and pushed through the hedge.

When she pushed out beside the book drop, she found Harry and his aunt standing there.

"We saw," Mrs. Flowers said, pointing to the newspaper tube Leeva had left in the hedge.

"We heard," Harry added.

"They left me here," Leeva said. The words sounded awful.

"They left you here," Mrs. Flowers confirmed. This time, the words did not sound quite so awful. On her face was a hint of Grateful Relief. It was so infinitesimal that only a person who had spent years studying facial expressions could hope to discern it, but Leeva was such a person.

"They left me here," she repeated, allowing a bit of her own Grateful Relief to show.

"We're here, too," Harry said.

Suddenly, Leeva wasn't the least bit tired. "I am here. And you are here!" she cried. Saying those words was even more satisfying than she had dreamed. And she knew exactly what to say next. "Want to move in? I have an elevator."

"To your parents' house?" Mrs. Flowers asked. "I don't think—"

"Oh, no!" Leeva assured her. "It's my house. My parents put the deed in my name, so that they never had to pay taxes. Each year, they tell me how much I owe and say, 'Ha! Good luck with that!'" She patted the pillow-case around her neck. "This should take care of it."

Well, Reader, it took only an hour to move every-thing from the little library apartment—including the toaster, Leeva made sure of that—into her house.

Mrs. Flowers took the room beside Leeva's, and Harry moved into the other bedroom. Once they were all in their pajamas they patted each other's heads and hugged each other as if they were precious—which they were—then went to bed.

Finally. Something that happened in her soap opera had happened to Leeva.

AT LAST

The next morning, Leeva rushed outside the instant she heard the *Nutsmore Weekly* thunk against the door. Force of habit. She didn't stop to pick up the paper, though. One of the things that Harry had moved the night before was the trimmer he used to keep the library's side of the hedge neat and smooth, and she had a couple of uses for that trimmer first.

She carried it to a spot on the hedge between the library's property and her own, and there she cut a wide, arched opening. Then she brought it back and set to work on the doorway briars, sawing and slashing until nothing stood in the way of anyone who wanted to visit. Satisfied, she sat on the step and opened the paper—today's word was bound to be extraordinary.

She flipped through the pages. She turned back to the beginning and flipped through again. And again.

Apparently, the paper was so stuffed with actual news from last night's events—"MAYOR AND TREASURER QUIT!" screamed the front page—that there'd been no room for the "Improve Your Vocabulary" column filler.

Leeva closed the paper and hung her head. She'd really, really wanted a new word, one worthy of this extraordinary week.

Just then, she heard the rumble of a large vehicle. It huffed to a stop, then she heard *beep-beep-beep* as it backed up.

Leeva dropped the paper and looked up. Through the wide arched opening in the hedge she saw an enormous truck parked in front of the library.

The new elevator! She collected Harry and his aunt and they all hurried over to watch as it was installed. Then they hung the Closed sign on the front doors and got to work.

The town reports got their own shelf up front where anybody could check them. Mrs. Flowers decided to dedicate the newly emptied top floor to cookbooks. "They're fiction and nonfiction both."

Up and down, up and down they rode.

At an urgent knocking on the front doors, Leeva let in the theater director, who asked for Harry.

"There was a New Voices scholarship in the budget," the director said, twirling his cape. "Ten thousand dollars. Because of your smash-hit play, we've voted to give it to you."

"Ten thousand dollars," Harry repeated, bracing himself against the elevator. "That's enough . . . It's exactly enough . . ."

Leeva patted his shoulder. "We'll miss you so much. But it's your destiny. Take thou thine clay, sculpt a stairway, all that, remember?"

"Once I get my knees fixed, we'll visit," his aunt promised.

Next, they drove to the courthouse to make their new family legal.

The courtroom was packed. Leeva marched up to Judge Hairball's bench confidently. "Those other two people were impersonators," she testified. Then she swung her arm around to Harry and Pauline, and came right out and said what she wanted. "I belong with *them*."

The judged banged her gavel. "Request granted!" she ruled, and the courtroom went bananas.

"Home?" Harry asked outside.

Home.

Leeva had always called it her *house* before.

She felt a familiar tingle. Maybe it wasn't exactly a new word, but it had a new definition now. And for the first time ever, she would use it on the same day she learned it.

"Yep!" she said with lots of oomph, plenty of pizzazz. "Home."